Submission Times Two

Claire Thompson

ISBN: 1-4392-4622-X
ISBN-13: 9781439246221

To order additional copies, please contact us.
BookSurge
www.booksurge.com
1-866-308-6235
orders@booksurge.com

chapter 1

ANDREW TOWNSEND STOOD in the shadows, watching. The man was standing, tethered and spread-eagled to the cross, wearing nothing but a codpiece. Positioned as he was, he appeared naked save for the thin belt of black leather over his narrow hips. The globes of his ass were well-defined, solid muscle, the indentations below either hip just begging to be gripped while a thick, hard cock was eased inside him.

His smooth body was covered in a sheen of sweat and the tendons on his neck were taut. His head was turned to the side and from where Andrew stood, he could see the man's face. The uninitiated might have only seen the pain, missing the underlay of ecstasy.

With each precisely aimed flick of the single-tail lash, the man's body jerked, the thickly corded muscles rippling just beneath the skin. Even in the dim light, Andrew could see the man had Viking white-blond hair curling down the back of his neck and falling over his eyes, which Andrew knew were ice blue.

A crowd had gathered around the carefully choreographed scene, the spectators respectfully silent in the face of people who actually knew what they were doing. Most of the guys there were just players. Men who cruised the sex bars and the underground BDSM clubs looking for one thing—the temporary thrill of a sexual power exchange with someone they didn't give a damn about and probably would never see again.

But from the scene he was watching, it was clear to Andrew these two were no players. As the single-tail struck again and again, leaving its thin, angry lines of pink over pale flesh, Andrew saw the change begin. The tensely bunched muscles of the man's strong back began to ease. His fingers uncurled and his head fell back, lips parting. A look of utter peace slid over his slackening features as he entered that elusive place where pleasure and pain lost their separate meanings.

Andrew's gut gripped and he realized he was clenching his fists. He should have been the one standing there wielding the whip. He should have been the one to take this sub to the heights of erotic pleasure.

He wanted to push through the crowd and knock the Dom out of the way. He wanted to put his arms around the bound man and kiss those lips he'd dreamed of for all these years. Watching the unfolding scene was like dousing Andrew's pent-up desire with gasoline and setting a match to it. He was burning out of control, his cock pressing like a steel rod in his jeans, jealousy dripping like an acid corroding his heart.

The Dom dropped the whip and moved forward to release the sub from the cuffs that held him bound at ankle and wrist. The sub leaned into him and slowly opened his eyes, offering a beatific smile that wrenched Andrew's soul.

The sub dropped to his knees and kissed the Dom's shiny black combat boots. The Dom leaned down, touching the top of his head like a priest bestowing a benediction.

Pushing his way past other scenes and the accompanying crowds, Andrew headed for the door, suddenly desperate for the fresh night air.

~*~

"Did you have fun last night?" Cam asked brightly as he set a plate of pancakes in front of Ethan. Ethan smiled at his lover. He never tired of looking at Cam's emerald green eyes, set off so perfectly by his mop of coppery auburn curls that fell in unruly tendrils around his face. He wore a small goatee that gave him a roguish, pirate look, a look that was heightened by the gold hoop in his right earlobe.

"That looks delicious. Thanks, Cam." Ethan poured syrup over the pancakes and took a bite. "Last night? It was fun, yeah. I got a good whipping with a single-tail from Master Richard. How about you? You were already asleep when I got in."

Cam shook his head, offering a rueful smile. "My night was pretty much a dud. The guy I was supposed to meet didn't show up, and I made the mistake of letting a guy I barely knew scene with me. He claimed to be an expert with the cane but after a few minutes, it was pretty clear he didn't know what the hell he was doing. And he was one of those verbal abuse guys, screaming at me to, 'shut the fuck up and take it, pussy boy!' I finally ended the scene."

"That sucks." Ethan reached over their small kitchen table and put his hand over Cam's. "Sometimes I wonder what the hell we're doing, Cam. I mean, we've got each other. Why do we go out looking for these guys who invariably end up disappointing us?"

"Because we had the bad sense to fall for each other and there isn't a guy out there who's Dom enough to handle us both."

Ethan laughed. "You can say that again. Jesus, nine out of ten guys I meet at these clubs are just posers."

Cam sighed. "Yeah. You're right. Maybe we should cancel our plans for tonight and just stay home and watch a movie."

Any other Saturday, Ethan would have agreed. Cam had been the one to suggest they go outside the relationship to get their submissive needs met. In the six months they'd been together before he'd had the idea, they'd tried to please each other, taking turns with the flogger and other toys they owned, but it hadn't worked out well. Neither of them had a dominant bone in his body, not when it came to sex. Each understood you couldn't fake being a Dom. It had to come from within, same as being sub. They would have certainly broken up by now if Cam hadn't come up with the idea of opening their relationship in the way they had.

So for the past five months, by explicit agreement, they'd divvied up the city, neither frequenting the BDSM clubs the other went to, at least not on the same night. They promised each other the scenes would not include sex, would always be at public clubs and would not involve their hearts.

So far it had worked pretty well. Each weekend they got their fill of cropping, caning, whipping, flogging and spanking, and then came home to each other, using their experiences to fuel the passion of their mostly vanilla lovemaking.

Normally, Ethan wouldn't have minded cancelling his plans for Cam, but not tonight. He was deeply intrigued by a new Dom he'd recently begun chatting with via email. He'd just appeared out of nowhere the week before, asking to be a friend on Ethan's Facebook.

They'd begun to chat and it had become clear after just a little while that Maestro was no player, but the real thing. At least, he said the right things and seemed genuine in his questions and responses. He was a romantic, like Ethan and Cam were, but also dominant—ready and willing to take control. He appreciated the need for a sub to experience erotic pain as a pathway to ecstasy. On the flipside, he too seemed to crave the intense connection such an experience could offer.

Add to that his photo, which showed a man with short brown hair, brown eyes and a large, hawkish nose. There was a strength in his features that Ethan found compelling. But it was the fire in his eyes that made Ethan's stomach drop. It was a whisper of a promise that bypassed Ethan's mind and spoke directly to his cock. Ethan couldn't stop staring at the photo.

Earlier in the week, Ethan had casually mentioned Maestro's emails to Cam, though he'd downplayed his own intense reaction. He didn't want to admit just how much he was looking forward to meeting Maestro face-to-face.

Keeping his tone light, Ethan said, "Any other night, I'd agree in a heartbeat. But remember that guy, Maestro, I was telling you about? I promised to meet him tonight at The Lair. If it's okay with you, I'd like to keep the date."

"Hey, that's cool. If you've got something worthwhile set up, go for it. If he's any good, wake me up when you get home and work off a little of that pent-up sexual energy, okay?"

Ethan reached over and ruffled Cam's luxuriant curls, love surging through him. "You got it, babe."

~*~

When Ethan got to the club, he went to the juice bar to wait for Maestro. Alcohol wasn't served at The Lair, a wise policy in a place where serious scenes took place. Ethan was early for his nine o'clock rendezvous—he never wanted to keep a Dom waiting. He ordered some lemonade and sipped absently at it while he waited, rejecting the occasional overture from guys looking to play. He kept glancing at his watch, willing the minute hand to reach the twelve.

At five of, someone touched his shoulder and Ethan swiveled on his stool. "You must be Ethan." Ethan found himself staring at the broad chest of a tall man. He looked upward into the long, angular face, caught by those large eyes, the color an unusual shade of coppery brown. The man's skin was rough and faintly pitted, as if he'd had acne in his youth, but instead of detracting from his looks, it only added to the ruggedness and power of his demeanor. His thick, dark hair was cut impeccably short. He had an old green Army duffel over his shoulder, no doubt filled with his toys for the evening.

Ethan stood and stepped back, extending his hand. "Yes. And you must be Maestro."

They shook hands. "One and the same." Maestro let his gaze settle on Ethan with an absorbing stare, as if he were memorizing Ethan's features for a later test.

Ethan felt suddenly self-conscious. He raised a hand to his cheek and rubbed at the blond stubble. "Uh, is everything okay?"

Maestro smiled, little more than the slight upturn at the corners of his lips. "Yes. I'm sorry if I'm staring. It's been so..." He cut himself off, but not before Ethan got the strange feeling he'd been about to say, "It's been so long."

"Have we met before? I think I'd remember if we'd shared a scene—"

"No, no," Maestro cut him off. "I'd remember that too, believe me." He signaled toward the bartender and ordered some grapefruit juice over crushed ice. "Let's find a table and talk."

"Sure."

Ethan followed the man, who looked to be about six foot, four inches tall. He was wearing black denim jeans that hugged his long, lean legs. He wore an untucked black button-down shirt that looked like silk.

The club, a converted warehouse on New York's Lower West Side, was laid out in a series of areas partitioned by sound-proofing panels to provide a modicum of privacy. Each space contained some of kind of equipment that lent itself to BDSM play—a whipping post, a set of stocks, a medical exam table, a rack, a St. Andrew's cross or simply a sturdy set of eyehooks in the ceiling, chains and cuffs dangling at the ready. Participants brought their own toys—whips, floggers, crops, ball gags, blindfolds, rope, chain, cuffs, paddles, clips and clamps. Club rules included no sexual intercourse, no exchange of bodily fluids and no full nudity. Other than that, pretty much anything was permitted.

The play areas were set in a circle around the bar floor, which contained a number of small tables, along with the counter set against one wall, swivel stools lining it. The place was fairly crowded, even at the relatively early hour of nine o'clock, but they found an empty table and sat down.

Maestro leaned back in his chair and again fixed Ethan with that searching gaze. "You mentioned in your emails that you're involved? You said it's an open relationship, but a committed one. I know we're just meeting for a scene, but I'd like to ask for a little more detail."

Ethan swallowed, realizing with a disconcerting jolt that this was the first time he'd ever felt the slightest hesitation in talking freely about Cam. "Yeah. I'm, uh, involved. It's kind of complicated." He smiled, wondering if Maestro would get it. "His name is Cam. We actually met at a club, but it turns out we're both sub. We hit it off really well and we tried to make a go of it. I mean, we're lovers and all that, but at first we tried to incorporate BDSM into our love life." He shrugged. "It just didn't work out. Two subs, playing at domming each other. We'd end up laughing more often than not."

Maestro nodded, again offering the hint of a smile. "So you go out to the clubs to get your kink needs met, while at home you're just vanilla lovers?"

Yeah, pretty much. We agreed we'd play outside the relationship with Doms, but only at public clubs and no sex."

"How's that working out for you? I imagine you'd need a pretty solid foundation to make something like that work. I mean, from our few emails, I got the sense you share my take on D/s. Even if you're not actually having sex, the emotional connection between a Dom and sub can be pretty intense, even," he paused, staring into Ethan's eyes, "intimate."

Ethan felt his face heat. He hadn't been this attracted to another man since Cam. A rush of guilt whipped through him at the strong sexual reaction the guy was provoking in him. He looked away, taking refuge in his glass. Sipping his lemonade, he tried to compose himself.

What the hell was wrong with him? Cam was the one he loved. Cam was the one he came home to after the BDSM play with men like Master James and Sir Tom. This was the first time in the eleven months he'd been with Cam that he found himself seriously entertaining the idea of having sex with another man.

The thought was deeply unsettling. In Cam he'd thought at last he'd found his life partner. Was he going to blow it with some guy he barely knew?

No fucking way.

Pushing his erotic fantasies down, he asserted with perhaps more vehemence than he'd intended, "Cam and I are in love. The BDSM play at the clubs is just for kicks."

It was Maestro's turn to look away. After a moment, he turned back, his mouth set in a thin line. "Fine. Works for me." He hefted his duffle bag onto his shoulder as he stood. "Let's have a few kicks."

~*~

You don't even know the guy anymore, so cut it out. Andrew admonished himself, refusing to admit how much Ethan's assertion of love for another hurt him. When they were emailing back and forth to set up their meeting, Andrew had been aware Ethan was involved but had assumed that wouldn't preclude their getting together for more than just a play scene at a public club.

He'd assumed that would just be the icebreaker, the first step toward seducing the guy who had been the fuel of Andrew's fantasies for so many years. He knew, too, if he were honest, that his continued obsession was based not on the man who stood before him, but on his own unrequited dreams, and a desire to get past the humiliations of high school.

They walked together to one of the empty spaces partitioned by the panels. The one they chose had chains hanging from the ceiling with leather cuffs attached. "We won't be needing those," Andrew announced. "You've assured me you're disciplined and can hold your position, correct?"

"Yes, Sir," Ethan said softly, his voice respectful.

They were in the scene, it was clear. No more small talk, no more negotiations. That had been done beforehand.

"Your safeword is…"

"Football."

Figures.

"I want to start with a full-body flogging. If I decide you're handling it well, we'll move on to the cane. Agreed?"

"Yes, Sir."

Andrew's cock was already hard in anticipation of whipping this gorgeous guy. Even if he hadn't known him from long ago, he would have been hot for the blond, sexy sub.

"Strip," he ordered.

Obediently, Ethan pulled his red T-shirt over his head, pushed the black leather sandals from his feet and stepped out of his jeans. He was wearing the same leather codpiece he'd worn the night before. It was made of soft leather, the outline of his semi-erect cock and balls visible beneath it, though they were completely covered.

Looking at it, Andrew decided it wasn't only decorative, but served as a kind of chastity belt, keeping errant hands from straying during a scene. This was probably a good thing, as Andrew doubted his own self-control to look at but not touch, given the opportunity.

"Hands behind your head. Stand at attention." Andrew set down his duffel bag and unzipped it, withdrawing a heavy flogger. He combed the leather tresses with his fingers, while watching Ethan get into position.

For a moment he thought about cuffing Ethan's wrists into the chains. He could unsnap the belt that held the codpiece in place and expose Ethan, who would be helpless to resist him. That would get his attention.

In high school Ethan Wise had been the effortlessly popular and quintessential jock. He was in the closet back then, not that anyone was particularly advertising their orientation at Walt Whitman High School in Hoboken, New Jersey back in 1994. But Ethan had taken it further. He had a girlfriend, as blonde and beautiful as himself, the cheerleader complement to the football player. Had he been using her purely as a front, or had he been that clueless about his own desires back then?

Whatever the case, Ethan could never have known about Andrew's secret yearnings. He was barely aware of, or at least indifferent to, the daily humiliations suffered by Andrew at the hands of Ethan's jock friends and hangers-on. As far as Andrew knew, Ethan hadn't known he was alive.

As the years passed, the acute pain of high school faded, relegated to a past that had little to do with the man Andrew was to become. He still thought about Ethan, but over time Ethan faded as a real person. He became instead that obscure object of desire, his image rising in Andrew's mind when he climaxed, his name sometimes nearly escaping Andrew's lips even when he was with another man. He was a fantasy and, until the email about the high school reunion, Andrew had thought that was all he could ever be.

Scrolling through his email one day a few weeks back, he'd very nearly deleted one from someone named Brenda Walker with the subject line: *Walt Whitman High School Class of 1994—Fifteen Year Reunion!* Through Brenda's Facebook, Andrew had tracked Ethan down.

Though he couldn't see Ethan's Facebook profile, Andrew's eyes widened in disbelief as he scrolled through the comments left by people with names that included, "sub boy hank", "Master Tyrell", "Sir Adam", "sissy boy", "James' fucktoy" and a host of others that left no doubt as to Ethan's sexual orientation and predilections.

Holy shit. Not only was Ethan gay, he was into the scene! Andrew had pondered this for a while, stunned by this unlikely and amazing turn of events. But was he Dom or sub? Unlike many of his Facebook friends, Ethan hadn't chosen to use a cute little moniker to indicate which end of the whip he preferred.

Andrew was determined to find out. For a moment, he moved the cursor over the, "Add as friend" icon next to Ethan's name on Brenda's friends page, but decided against it. While the thought of connecting with the adult Ethan was very exciting, he didn't want to enter the situation at a disadvantage.

Reappearing in Ethan's life as Andy, the loser geek from Walt Whitman, would be a decided disadvantage. And so Andrew signed out of his own Facebook account and created a new one, choosing the name of *Maestro*.

He created a profile describing himself as gay and into the BDSM scene. Along with a headshot of himself, he posted photos of some of his favorite toys—a heavy, black suede flogger, a bamboo cane, a pair of clover clamps, the spreader bar he'd made himself from a few dollars worth of wood and eyehooks at Home Depot and a very sexy picture of a bound, naked man, kneeling in submission in front of a man wearing black leather pants tucked into black boots.

Signed in as Maestro, Andrew did a new search on Ethan Wise, found him and clicked a request to be added as his friend. To his delight, within less than twenty-four hours Ethan had accepted his request.

Ethan's Facebook revealed a man heavily involved in the scene and most definitely submissive. Andrew was surprised he was friends with Brenda—did he no longer care what those jocks back at high school thought? If he ever got to know him better, he'd have to find out.

If they got past this one scene, that is. Now Andrew lifted the flogger and moved to stand just behind Ethan. He dragged the tresses over Ethan's strong shoulders and down his back, pleased to note the small tremor of anticipation that moved through Ethan's body.

No, he wouldn't cuff him. He would take Ethan's measure by flogging him and caning him, observing his reactions and deciding if he was worthy of Maestro's continued attentions. He would put the fantasy of one day meeting and falling in love with, or more accurately having Ethan fall in love with him, behind him once and for all.

He was a grown man. It was time to move on. He'd take what he could get, which in this case promised to be a very hot scene with a very hot guy.

He stepped closer behind Ethan until his clothed chest was touching Ethan's bare back. With his free hand, he reached around and found Ethan's right nipple, which he rolled between forefinger and thumb until it hardened. He twisted it, drawing a slight gasp from the sub, though he remained still and in position.

Unable to resist, Andrew brushed his erect cock against Ethan's ass. To his surprise, Ethan pushed back, wriggling against Andrew's shaft. "Stay still, slut," Andrew barked, though inside he was thrilled.

Ethan stilled at once and Andrew stepped back. He walked around to face Ethan, raking his eyes over his face and sweeping lower. Ethan's cock was fully erect now, pressing hard against the soft leather of the codpiece.

"Are you ready to suffer for me?" Andrew returned his gaze to Ethan's face, pleased to note the flush on his cheeks and the shining look of anticipation in his light blue eyes.

"Yes, Sir."

chapter 2

ETHAN STARED UP into Maestro's face, hypnotized by his brooding eyes. "Eyes straight ahead, sub boy," Maestro snapped and Ethan at once dropped his gaze. His right nipple still throbbed from the savage twist Maestro had given it. His left nipple ached for the touch it hadn't received. His cock was bent uncomfortably in the leather codpiece, his balls tightening with desire.

Something about this man emanated sensuality and oozed sexual power. It was a rare Dom who could arouse him so quickly.

Much more commonly, when he engaged in play with men he met at these clubs, that's all it was—playing. The bondage and erotic torture was limited by the venue. It was mutual masturbation, but without the orgasm. That would come later, at home with Cam.

And until this moment that had suited Ethan just fine. It was the primary reason Cam and he agreed only to meet Doms at these public clubs. That way not only were they safe from a possibly overzealous guy, but they didn't run the risk of succumbing to any possible temptation.

It wasn't that they didn't trust one another. It was that they both understood the power of a D/s interaction. Something changed in a sub's psyche when he was bound and subject to the sharp, sweet kiss of leather against bare skin. If the person wielding the whip knew what he was doing, a good whipping was as intense as any lovemaking. Certainly it was as intimate.

Maestro was standing behind and just to the side of him. Ethan wanted to turn and look at him, but he knew better than to move out of position. "Bend forward, stick out your ass. Offer it to me," Maestro commanded. His voice was deep and confident, commanding obedience. Ethan pushed his ass out, the skin tingling in anticipation of the flogger.

He was surprised to feel Maestro's bare hand moving over his ass, cupping and squeezing the flesh. He resisted the impulse to push back against it, as he had against Maestro's erection.

A sudden sharp slap to his left cheek pulled a gasp of startled pain from Ethan's lips. It was followed by a second slap, just as hard, to his right. Ethan loved a good, hard spanking, perhaps even more than a flogging. He stuck his ass out farther, hoping for a repeat visit by that very hard palm.

Instead, leather dragged its way over his flesh, the tips nearly tickling him as they glided from his ass over his back. He was ready when Maestro began to flog him lightly, the leather slapping against his back, ass and thighs with a satisfying sound.

The Dom clearly knew what he was doing, covering Ethan's skin from shoulder to thigh with the leather, preparing it for what was to come. Soon the sound of Ethan's breathing mingled with the raining song of the leather against skin.

The soft brush of the flogger became steadily harder, its sensual, stinging caress easing Ethan farther into erotic pain with each new stroke. "Ah," he cried out involuntarily when Maestro struck especially hard. The tresses of the flogger covered both ass cheeks, the tips curling cruelly around Ethan's hip.

Ethan closed his eyes, his head falling back, though he remained in position with his fingers laced behind his head. Maestro was bringing him quickly to the pinnacle of the erotic pain. Would he be able to begin the slow, perfect glide into that slice of heaven where the sting shifted from something nearly intolerable to something he never wanted to stop?

Though he'd learned over the years to give himself fully to the pain and let it draw him to the pleasure, it wasn't something he could do alone. It required the skill of a masterful Dom to take him there. Even if a Dom was reasonably adept at handling a whip, there was more at play. The Dom had to know when to stop, but more importantly, when to keep going.

Maestro kept going.

Ethan was aware of the sound of someone's ragged panting before he realized it was his own. "Slow your breathing," Maestro said, leaning so close his warm breath tickled Ethan's ear. "Flow with it. Slow down. Take your time."

Ethan attempted to obey, drawing a deep, shuddery breath and letting it out as slowly as he could. The flogger struck again, the blow so forceful Ethan gasped and nearly fell forward before managing to right himself.

"Breathe through it, breathe past it," Maestro whispered. He continued to flog Ethan's back, ass and thighs, striking him hard. Ethan was forced to tense his muscles to keep from being knocked out of position by the blows.

It hurt, the pain ratcheting to where Ethan could barely tolerate it. "Please," he managed, through gritted teeth. He knew he was seconds away from toppling, if he permitted himself to let go. "I can't...I can't..."

"You can. You are. You're right there, Ethan. Let go." Ethan was standing on his toes, his interlocked fingers pressing hard against his head. He *wanted* to let go—to fly away to that perfect, elusive place where nothing existed but the powerful alloy of pleasure and pain.

"You're resisting," Maestro said softly, and Ethan knew it was true. He desperately wanted what Maestro was offering, what was being held tantalizingly close, if only he could find the submissive trust to seize it.

That's when he realized what was going on. It wasn't that he didn't trust Maestro. He didn't trust himself. If he flew with this man, what would happen next? If he were this involved, this connected, just from one flogging session, how could he hope to keep his promise to Cam?

"I can't," he said again, dropping his arms and wrapping them around his torso. "I'm sorry. I can't."

Maestro stepped back, knitting his brow. "I don't understand. You were so close. I know you were. Let me take you there. You know you need it—"

"No!" Ethan cut him off sharply. "I said I can't. The scene is over."

Maestro flinched and dropped his arm, the flogger dangling limply from his hand. Without a word, he retrieved his duffel bag and pushed the flogger into it, his face averted. Ethan held back the urge to drop to his knees, wrap his arms around Maestro's legs and beg his forgiveness.

Maestro turned back, his expression blank. "I'm sorry," he said stiffly. "I misgauged your responses. I should have taken you more slowly."

Ethan didn't reply. Maestro hadn't misgauged or misread. A few more well-placed strokes would have sent him over the edge—he would have lost control. He would have given himself, not just his body, but his heart, to this tall, handsome stranger.

"I'm sorry. It's my fault," Ethan tried. "It's just...I can't..."

"It's okay. It was our first time. I shouldn't have pushed so hard. It's not your fault. I was the one running the scene. I guess I wasn't reading you correctly." He hoisted his duffel bag over his shoulder and turned away. "Maybe another time."

"Wait," Ethan said urgently. Maestro again turned toward him, raising his eyebrows in question. "It's just..." Ethan paused, wondering how much to give away. "You didn't do anything wrong. It's me. I was so close. I was about to fly."

Maestro turned to face him fully. "I know. That's what I don't get. Isn't that the point?"

Ethan knew his cheeks were coloring. "Yeah. I guess. But with you, I don't know..." *I wanted you. Not just it, not just the experience of flying, but you.* Maestro waited, his head cocked slightly to the side. "I—I think I wanted it too much."

"I don't understand."

Ethan licked his lips and tried again. "I have someone. You know. I told you about Cam."

"Yes. Your lover." Maestro seemed to almost stumble over the word. It suddenly occurred to Ethan that he knew nothing about Maestro's private life. Not that Maestro knew so much about his, but their talks online and on the phone had focused on Ethan and what his expectations and limits were.

What about Maestro? Did he have someone at home? A vanilla partner, perhaps, who sent him off to the clubs to get his jollies? Ethan wanted to know this man better. Not just as a Dom, but as a person.

He reached for his clothing, piled in a corner of the small enclosure. "Can we go back to the bar and talk? I feel like I need to process whatever just happened."

Maestro's stony façade fell away and for a split second Ethan saw the longing there. What was going on? Who was this guy? Was he as into whatever had happened as Ethan had been? Ethan found himself suddenly terrified at the prospect of opening whatever dangerous can of worms now existed between them.

What about his darling Cam, waiting dutifully at home for his trusted lover to return? Swallowing hard, Ethan backtracked. "I'm sorry. I don't know what I was thinking. I have to be somewhere. But let's stay in touch, okay? The scene was awesome. You were great. I was just…I don't know. Not ready."

Maestro watched Ethan dress, his face settling into impassive lines, his eyes hooded and opaque. "Sure, yeah. I'll see you around."

And with that, he was gone.

~*~

"The prodigal son returns." Cam smiled toward Ethan as he came through the door of their small Brooklyn apartment. His heart never failed to miss a beat each time he saw his lover after a time apart, even as little as a few hours. Strong, muscular body, white-blonde hair, firm jaw, aquiline nose, ready smile. But it was his eyes that captivated Cam anew every time he looked into them.

The irises were a clear, light blue, but if you looked closely, the blue was flecked with bits of white, like tiny diamonds that caught and reflected the light. His lashes were thick and long, the color of spun gold. Cam loved nothing better than to lie in Ethan's arms after sex and just lose himself in those beautiful eyes.

Ethan was older by five years to Cam's twenty-eight, but in some ways he was less experienced, especially when it came to D/s. Cam had, albeit briefly, been the live-in sub of a very intense Dom named Bryan quite a few years before hooking up with Ethan.

The Dom/sub component of their relationship had been very intense and, at first, all-consuming. No matter how much Cam gave of himself, it was never enough for his Master. Bryan took control of everything Cam did, down to when he used the toilet, how much he could eat, when and where he could sleep. Constantly stimulated, sexually aroused and erotically tortured, Cam found himself losing his identity as a separate person. He was literally being brainwashed and sexually conditioned to obey Bryan's every whim.

They'd been together six weeks when he'd come to his senses. It was the day Bryan had calmly informed Cam he'd called Cam's boss and told him Cam wouldn't be coming back to work. He was going to devote himself 24/7 to being Bryan's private slave. Bryan saw nothing wrong with what he'd done.

Furthermore, he told Cam he was going to chain him down that night and brand him with his mark of permanent ownership.

Cam had moved out that afternoon.

After a six-month hiatus from the scene, he'd returned to the underground clubs, no longer certain of what he wanted when it came to D/s. When he'd finally met Ethan, the physical attraction was immediate, but it was more than that. They'd connected instantly, talking as if they'd known each other for years, instead of minutes.

Ethan had taken Cam home that very first night, both of them laughing ruefully over the fact neither was Dom. At least, they told each other, they shared the same romantic worldview about D/s and BDSM. They'd find a way, they told each other, to make it work for them.

Sometimes he worried a little about their arrangement, though he was the one who had come up with it. Ethan took advantage of their open policy regarding play with Doms at clubs more frequently than Cam did. Was he unwittingly sending Ethan off into the arms of another?

Cam, too, adored the kiss of the lash and the command of a strong Dom, but he didn't *require* it in quite the same way Ethan seemed to. Still, Cam wasn't a jealous man by nature, and he trusted Ethan. So far, their arrangement had worked out pretty well. Ethan loved him and he loved Ethan.

Cam had been lounging on the sofa in his pajama bottoms watching a movie while he waited for Ethan to get home. He held up his bowl. "I wasn't expecting you so early. Want some popcorn?"

Ethan came over and sat heavily beside him. "No, thanks. Not hungry."

Cam paused the movie and turned to face Ethan. "So how did it go with that guy, Maestro? Was he the real thing? I figured you wouldn't be home before midnight at the earliest."

"He was…it was…okay." Ethan's face was in shadow.

"That good, huh?" Cam teased.

Ethan turned and looked at Cam head-on, those vivid blue and diamond eyes piercing into his. "I love you, Cam. You know that, right?"

Cam smiled, Ethan's words at once warming and unnerving him. "Sure. I know that. I love you too."

Ethan stared at him a while longer and finally nodded slowly. "Good. That's good then." He reached for the popcorn, scooping a buttery handful into his mouth as he turned toward the TV screen. "What're you watching?"

Ignoring the question for a moment, Cam said, "Tell me about tonight. What happened? What's got you all freaked out?"

"What?" Ethan whipped his head toward Cam. "What makes you think I'm freaked out? I'm fine. Just tired, is all. The night was fine. The guy had a really heavy, thuddy flogger—"

"My favorite," Cam interjected.

Ethan offered a small smile. "Yeah. He knew how to use it, too."

"So it was good? You're ready for me now?" Cam kept his tone light. He put his hand on Ethan's thickly-muscled thigh and slid it toward his crotch. "He warmed you up for a good fucking?"

Ethan's eyes slid away and he turned his head. Cam's gut clenched. What the hell was going on? Removing his hand from Ethan's thigh, Cam reached for Ethan's chin, forcing him to look at him. Whatever was going on, he had to know.

"What is it, Ethan? Talk to me. Please?"

Ethan pulled away from Cam's grasp. He stood and smiled, holding out his hand. "Hey, nothing. It's nothing, really. And yeah, I'm definitely ready for a good fucking. Though I was thinking of fucking you first, if that's okay, Mr. McNamee."

Cam stared hard at Ethan, searching his face, but Ethan only smiled more broadly. "Hey, really. It's cool. Come on. Let's go to bed." He continued to hold out his hand until Cam reached for it, allowing Ethan to pull him up. He flicked off the movie and set the bowl of popcorn on the coffee table.

Ethan pulled him into his arms and nuzzled his head against Cam's neck. "You're the one I love. You."

Cam held him, trying hard to ignore the chill this emphatic assertion sent through his blood.

~*~

Andrew left the club. He needed a bar that offered something more than juice and soda. The Lair was located on Fourteenth Street, not too far from Christopher Street and Andrew's favorite local gay bar, Justine's.

He barely noticed the passersby jostling him along the wide, crowded sidewalks as he walked. In his head, he was still back at The Lair in the small, partitioned area, flogging the sexy, hard body of the man he'd secretly fantasized about for the last fifteen years.

A part of him had expected to be let down—indeed, he now realized, had hoped to be let down. He would share a scene with Ethan Wise and Ethan would reveal himself as a player, a poser, a wannabe and Andrew would get over him, once and for all.

But that hadn't happened.

What the hell *had* happened?

Ethan was physical perfection, his body all sinew and muscle, the body of a lifetime athlete. Andrew's first impulse, rather than to flog such beauty, was to lick his way over the smooth supple skin and bury his nose in the tufts of blond hair at his armpits. He wanted to rip that leather codpiece from Ethan's body and take his shaft deep into his throat. He wanted to possess Ethan, not merely as a Dom, but as a lover.

Instead he stayed carefully within the confines of their agreed-upon scene, waiting to see how Ethan handled a real whipping. Forgetting his own wish that Ethan fail him so he could move on with his life, he'd been entranced by Ethan's strong response.

Just watching from the shadows the night before, he'd known Ethan could take a whipping, but he hadn't counted on the intense, visceral connection he'd felt when he'd been the one to wield the whip. It had happened only a few times in his life, and certainly not the first time out with someone.

Ethan took each stroke, succumbing to the stinging insistence of the flogger with the grace and honesty of a true submissive. The connection between them for those few minutes had been about more than a physical attraction, more than a shared love of the scene.

Andrew had taken Ethan farther and faster than perhaps he should have. But he'd been so sure of the path. It had been so natural, so right, to do it. A few more strokes, just a few more and Ethan would have entered that special place—that heady, powerful zone only the combination of pain and lust could produce in a man who was hardwired as Ethan was.

Andrew had never personally flown, as it was termed, but he'd witnessed and induced it enough to understand something of its power. When he was the one to bring that change over someone with his hands, his whip, his words, the power rush was incredible. It was as if he were holding tight to the string of a kite being tossed in high winds. It was up to him to keep it steady and sure in its flight. He had to gauge just how far to push and when to pull back and ease off. It was a dance that took skill and intuition. It was one he thought he knew the steps to.

But tonight, just as Ethan stood perched and ready to soar, he'd stopped the scene. At first Andrew had been completely bewildered. What had he missed? What had he done wrong?

Then he'd realized what Ethan was trying to say. It was about his lover. The man named Cameron who waited at home for him. He didn't want to fly because flying was too intense, too special to be shared with the likes of Andrew. No, all Ethan had wanted from Andrew, or Maestro, as he knew him, was a good flogging. Maestro was nothing more than a tool, when you really got down to it, preparing Ethan to go home to his lover for the real interaction.

The dumb thing was, Andrew knew this going in. He'd agreed to the terms as stated—no sex, just a scene, cut and dry, pure and simple. But he hadn't counted on Ethan's strong reaction. He hadn't counted on his own fierce response. He hadn't counted on Ethan's ending things before Andrew was able to truly take control.

Because that was the crux, wasn't it? If he were honest, in his heart of hearts, beyond all the bullshit he tried to tell himself about getting over Ethan by finally sharing a scene, his real plan from the outset was to seduce him. To steal him away from the guy waiting at home. To give him such an intense D/s experience he wouldn't be able to help falling in love, at least a little, with his Dom.

But that hadn't happened.

Instead Ethan had ended the scene and sent Maestro on his way, lonelier than he'd been when he started. What the hell was wrong with him? There were plenty of sub boys he could snap his fingers at who would come running.

Just like back in high school, the game had ended before it was played and the score was Ethan one, Andrew zero.

chapter 3

ANDREW MANAGED TO drown his sorrows at Justine's, though he'd warded off the attempts of several guys more than willing to help him forget completely. He just wasn't in the mood.

Sunday was spent running errands and cleaning his apartment, preparing himself for the workweek ahead. He'd checked his email a dozen times, but had heard nothing from Ethan. He'd composed and then deleted several emails demanding an explanation for Ethan's abrupt ending of the scene, but pride had prevented him from sending them. Pride and the lesson he'd learned not to send off emails in the heat of the moment filled with things he'd regret later. If he did write, it would be after a little more time had passed and hopefully a little more perspective was gained.

Throughout the day and on into the night, he had a running argument with himself. Here he'd finally met the guy he'd dreamed of for so long and just like that, he'd let him slip through his fingers.

He shouldn't have backed down so easily. Ethan was a true sub, that much was made clear by his strong, even ardent reaction to the flogging. Andrew knew he'd done the right thing in stopping at Ethan's insistence, but he shouldn't have let him go so easily. He should have taken the time to find out the reason for Ethan's abrupt withdrawal. He should have stood his ground. He should have given Ethan at least a hint of his true feelings.

Instead he'd run, burned by Ethan's rejection and afraid of his own feelings for a man who was admittedly in love with someone else.

The awful thing was, he still wanted him. He wanted the real man more than he'd wanted the fantasy, the memory of the boy he'd known in high school. And damn it, he had *had* him for a few precious moments, but he'd let him slip away.

Andrew was glad on Monday for the distraction of his work. He was in the thick of a complex project that required all his attention so that, at least for a while, he could forget about Ethan Wise. He was just working out the details of a sticky piece of the design when his cell phone began to vibrate in his jacket pocket. He ignored it, aware that if he stopped now, he'd lose his train of thought. After a moment the vibration ceased and he soon forgot all about the missed call.

A half-hour later, the hurdle in the design cleared, he reached into his jacket pocket, pulled out the phone and flipped it open.

Ethan Wise's name scrolled across the screen. Ethan! He saw there was also a voicemail. His heart thumping, he punched the one on the keypad, holding it down to call his voicemail.

"Hi, uh, Maestro?" Ethan offered a nervous laugh. "You know, I don't even know your real name. But, um, well, I was wondering. Things ended kind of strange between us the other night. I felt bad about it." A short pause, and then, "You mentioned you work in the city. My office is on Fifth Avenue. I'm pretty flexible if you wanted to maybe meet for coffee or lunch or something? I mean, no pressure, but I, uh, I was hoping we could talk some more. Face-to-face. Let me know, okay? Thanks, bye."

Andrew flipped the phone shut and stared out the window of his office building. Jumping up, he began to pace his office. Ethan wanted to see him again! Even if it was just to apologize, this was his chance. He could be on Fifth Avenue in ten minutes, if he took a taxi.

Flipping the phone open again, he called Ethan, who picked up the phone almost instantly. "Maestro? Hi. I recognized the number. I'm glad you called back."

Andrew's cock stiffened at the sound of Ethan's voice. He forced nonchalance into his voice. "Yeah, sorry I missed your call. I was kind of involved in something on the computer that took all my concentration."

"Hey, no problem. So you got my message?"

"Yeah. I'm glad you called. I've—I've been thinking about you." *Understatement of the year.*

"I've been thinking about you too," Ethan said. "Way too much."

Andrew's heart skipped a beat at this admission. He glanced at the blueprints spread over his desk and the computer code on his screen. Could he afford to get away? He laughed at himself, aware he'd already made the decision.

Keeping his voice as neutral as possible, he said, "I could meet you somewhere. Say, one o'clock? Would that work for you?"

"Sure. I could pick you up. I drove in today from Brooklyn because I have to go out to see a client on Staten Island at three. So one o'clock is perfect. Where do you work?"

"Stratton Engineering, on West 35th." He gave Ethan directions and they said their goodbyes. He still hadn't offered his real name and Ethan hadn't pressed. Just as well. No reason for Ethan to associate him with the geeky Andy of the bad old days.

Somehow he made it through the next two hours, eating a sandwich at his desk while he worked on his designs, finally becoming so absorbed he forgot about Ethan, at least for a while. He was startled by the cell phone's vibration, surprised it was one o'clock already.

"Hi," Ethan said. "I'm double-parked in front of your building."

"Oh, sorry. I didn't realize it was so late. I'll be right down."

Ethan was waiting in a cherry red Prius, a smile on his handsome face. Andrew climbed into the car and Ethan eased his way into the traffic. "Hey. You look good in a suit and tie," Ethan offered, giving Andrew an appraising look.

Andrew looked down at himself, suddenly self-conscious. "Corporate persona, what can I say?" He looked Ethan over in turn. Ethan was wearing faded blue jeans and a blue and white striped cotton button-down shirt, untucked. It hugged his broad shoulders and tapered down to his narrow waist. "You look pretty damn hot yourself. I wish we had your dress code at my company."

"Yeah. We have it pretty good. I work for a small web design outfit called Blue Diamond Media. It was started by a guy named Roger Hicks who left Microsoft to start his own company. He has that whole keep-the-workspace-creative mentality. We have a pool table, unlimited free pizza and soda, no dress code and no set hours. Some people don't come in till noon but they might work till three in the morning if they're on a project. I love working there. I'm really lucky to have landed the job."

"Sounds like. I wouldn't have imagined you working in something like web design."

"What do you mean? Why not?"

"Well, with the football and all." Andrew bit his tongue. Rapidly he scoured his brain, trying to remember if Ethan had ever mentioned his high school football career, either on his Facebook or during their chats.

Ethan shot him a sidelong glance and then looked back toward the road. "Football?"

I should tell him who I am, Andrew thought, but he couldn't figure out how to approach it without coming across like a total jerk. Instead, he lied. "Yeah, I remember you mentioned something about football when we were first talking. Or maybe I'm confused."

"No, no. I did actually play football back in high school, but I don't remember mentioning it is all. I don't talk about those days much. All I can say is thank god they're behind me. High school totally sucked."

Andrew stared at Ethan in open disbelief. What the hell was this guy talking about? Ethan Wise was king of the world back then, the most popular guy in the class. To cover his surprise, he said, "I would have thought someone like you, so good-looking and athletic, would have had it made in high school."

Ethan retorted, "Are you kidding me? I was so deep in the closet I couldn't even find myself half the time. I was so busy desperately trying to please everyone around me, from my dad, who was hell bent on me making a career in sports, to my mom, who was eagerly waiting for those grandchildren I was going to provide as soon as I married her choice of daughter-in-law, to the jocks who called themselves my friends but whom I had nothing in common with except sports, to my various girlfriends, who wondered why I had such a hard time getting it up for them."

Ethan laughed bitterly. "I never even kissed a guy until senior year of college. I spent the first twenty-one years of my life living a lie."

Andrew sat stunned as he absorbed this information. It had never occurred to him the cost for Ethan of pretending to be straight, or how long Ethan had been able to perpetrate the lie. He looked at Ethan with new eyes, for the first time feeling not only lust and unrequited desire, but also compassion.

Forgetting to censor himself, he shook his head, murmuring, "Homecoming King, president of the student council, captain of the football team. And it turns out you were just as miserable as the rest of us."

As soon as he said it, he realized what he'd done. What an ass. Ah, well. It was done. It had only been a matter of time, anyway. He would have had to admit it sooner or later. Still, he felt sick with apprehension. Leaning back, he closed his eyes and waited for the other shoe to fall.

"What the hell?" Ethan demanded, as if on cue. "Who *are* you? How do you know about my life back in high school? I *know* I didn't tell you all *that*." Ethan pressed his foot on the brake, stopping at the red light and turning his sharp gaze to Andrew.

Shrugging in defeat, aware he was blushing, Andrew admitted, "I'm Andrew Townsend. We went to high school together. You probably don't remember me. I used to be called Andy."

~*~

Ethan slid into a parking spot on the side of the street. They weren't yet at the coffee shop he'd been heading for, but he was no longer in the mood for coffee. This was too strange. Way too strange.

Once parked, he unbuckled his seatbelt and turned to face Maestro, or rather, Andrew. There was no way this tall, handsome, sexy man was Andy, the short, pimply-faced nerd who jumped any time anyone said his name. He stared at Andrew, trying to reconcile this man with his vague memories of that boy, the one his jock friends had derisively called a faggot.

"*You're* Andy from Walt Whitman High?"

"Andrew. I go by Andrew now. But yeah. One and the same, though like you, I prefer to put those bad old days behind me."

Ethan continued to stare at him, unable to stop himself. "But you look so different. I mean..." He cut himself off, biting his lip, aware how this must sound.

"Yeah. You don't have to couch it. I know what I looked like back then. I got all that long, greasy hair cut off the summer after senior year. My skin cleared up freshman year of college, and I started to grow and didn't stop until I'd put on seven inches. I joined the college swim team too. That got me in shape, I guess. I've continued to swim ever since. I find it very relaxing."

That explains your gorgeous bod, Ethan thought, though he didn't say that aloud. He didn't know what the hell to think about this bizarre turn of events. Clearly Maestro, or rather Andrew, had some explaining to do. In a way, this was a relief. Ethan could focus on Andrew's deception instead of his own internal conflicts.

"I'm still trying to get my head around this. The whole thing's pretty weird. It's like, I don't know, what are you, some kind of stalker or something?"

"God, no! It's not like that. Not at all." Andrew pursed his lips and stared out the car window. Ethan waited, refusing to cut him any slack, curious to see how he'd talk himself out of this one. Andrew continued. "This is really embarrassing. It's not how you think. I mean, I wasn't, like, following you around secretly or anything weird like that. I know I should have told you sooner. I guess the truth is, I didn't want you to associate me as I am now with the kid I was back then.

"I was going to tell you when we met face-to-face but when I saw you, I forgot everything but the moment..." He trailed off, but then added, "I wasn't expecting the scene between us to be so...intense. Nor, to be honest, did I expect you to run off the way you did."

It was Ethan's turn to be embarrassed. Not quite ready to face that issue, he brought the focus back to Andrew's deception. "Yeah, well. I'm not sure how I feel about all this. I don't know. I don't know what to think."

Anguish washed over Andrew's face and he blew out a long breath. "I'm sorry," he said in a low voice. He pushed his fingers through his close-cropped hair and offered a wan smile. "Man, I haven't felt this awkward or stupid since high school. I'm not really sure how to make this right." He unbuckled his seatbelt and put his hand on the door handle. For a moment Ethan thought he was going to get out of the car.

Instead he turned back to Ethan, new resolution in his voice. "Okay, listen. I'll just tell you straight out what went down. Then you make your own decisions." Ethan nodded, waiting. Andrew continued. "I got an invitation from Brenda somebody for the high school reunion. No fucking way was I going to *that*." Andrew did manage a smile now, and Ethan smiled back in spite of himself, nodding in agreement. "But I saw your name on the list of friends on her Facebook and it got me to thinking. You see..."

"I see...what?"

Andrew gave a small laugh. "I hadn't planned on admitting this, but I know I owe you an explanation, so here goes. Back then I was hopelessly, utterly and totally in love with you from afar."

"What?" Whatever Ethan had expected, that hadn't been it. "With *me?*"

"Are you *kidding? Yes,* with you. Why should I be different from half the student population? You were the hottest guy in the school, without question."

"I had no idea…"

"Of course you had no idea. Why the hell would you? You were off in your bubble, surrounded by your popular friends and the girls who wrote you love letters in class. You probably weren't even aware I existed, except as an object of derision in the locker room where I was usually to be found getting my pants pulled down or my head shoved into a toilet."

Andrew snapped his mouth shut and Ethan saw he was clenching his fists in his lap. Impulsively, Ethan put his hand on Andrew's thigh and squeezed it, his heart aching with sympathy. He'd been aware of the systematic harassment Andy and other openly gay kids had endured at the hands of a few Neanderthal jocks, but he'd never tried to stop them. Instead he'd distanced himself, too concerned with his own cover to make waves. Shame washed over him now at the boy he'd been in high school.

"I'm sorry, Andy…uh, Andrew. I'm sorry for everything from those bad old days. I guess I can see why you didn't tell me up front who you were."

Relief shone on Andrew's face. "I appreciate that." After a moment he chuckled. "You sure put up a good front. Shit, if I'd known you were gay, I'd have tracked you down ages ago. I just assumed you were straight. For all I knew, you were married with two kids. Until I saw your name there, and tracked you down on Facebook, I had no idea you were gay or into the scene."

Ethan studied Andrew's handsome face, staring into his deep brown eyes. He shook his head, still caught up in memories of high school. "You know, it's ironic. I was the popular one, with the good grades and the football and the girls, but I was living a lie. Whatever you had to go through, at least you had the courage of your convictions."

Andrew smiled. "Thank you, Ethan. It means a lot to me to hear you say that. Still, I should have told you up front. I guess I wanted to meet you on my own terms, as I am now. Then, when we did connect, and you told me you had a significant other at home—that if we met it had to be a public club and with strict rules for our play, well, I thought I could handle it. I didn't count on your being even better looking now than when we were kids. I didn't count on your incredible submissive grace when we played...When you ended things so abruptly, I tried to rationalize it in my head. To remind myself you were in a committed relationship and this was just as well. But I was lying, Ethan. I wanted you, bad." His voice trailed to a whisper. "I still do."

And I want you. Ethan didn't say the words aloud. He hadn't said them to anyone but Cam for nearly a year.

They were both quiet for several moments. Andrew broke the silence. "Ethan. Why did you want to see me again?"

Ethan didn't answer at once. He hadn't been entirely sure of his own motives in seeing the Dom again. A part of him knew it was a mistake. His heart belonged to Cam and by seeing Maestro, or Andrew, or whoever the hell this guy was, he was breaking his promise to Cam to only see Doms at public clubs, and then only for the play scenes they engaged in.

Yet he hadn't been able to get Maestro out of his head. It was affecting his relationship with Cam, who had become aware over the course of the weekend that something was bothering Ethan, though Ethan refused to admit it. He didn't want to hurt Cam by revealing how strong his reaction had been toward Maestro and the intense connection they'd forged in such a brief time. He'd hoped his feelings would fade as the days passed, but he found himself thinking about it more and more.

While he did love Cam with all his heart, he needed a Dom. He needed a Dom in his life, not just for play, but for real. The realization was deeply disturbing, because it meant the beginning of the end with Cam, and yet there it was.

With no idea what to do about it, Ethan had thought of Maestro. He seemed so sure and confident, and so knowledgeable about D/s. Ethan thought maybe he'd give him some advice. Maybe he'd show him what to do.

Ethan knew he was lying to himself, or not being fully truthful. Yes, he was hoping Maestro could guide him, but more than that, he just flat out wanted to see him again. He wanted to feel the touch of his fingers gliding over bare skin, the kiss of his whip, the press of his lips...

Ethan turned to face Andrew and felt himself being pulled as if by some magnetic force he was powerless to resist. "I—I couldn't stop thinking about you..." he whispered. Andrew was watching him, his eyes burning as he too leaned toward Ethan. With silent collusion, their lips met. Andrew's kiss became more insistent. He slid his tongue into Ethan's mouth while pulling him closer with a hand on the back of Ethan's neck.

Ethan forgot Cam in that moment. He forgot his promises. He forgot his conflicts. He forgot that Andrew had lied to him by omission and he forgot to be put off and confused by that. All he knew was this kiss mustn't stop. He touched Andrew's face with his fingers and let himself be lost in that long, perfect kiss, oblivious of everything around them.

When they finally pulled apart, Ethan fell back against the car door, trying to catch his breath. His heart was pounding like hoofbeats on stone, his cock straining in his jeans. Andrew's eyes were glittering. He lifted his large hand and cupped Ethan's crotch.

"Whatever the hell's going on between us, Ethan, I know I don't want it to stop."

Neither, god help me, do I, thought Ethan, even as Cam's open, sunny face inserted itself like a silent reproach into his mind.

chapter 4

CAM STEPPED BACK and eyed the painting with an appraising eye. Stepping forward again, he tilted the frame a fraction of an inch and stepped back again. Satisfied it was straight, he gave the small gallery a sweeping gaze, trying to see it with fresh eyes. He wasn't quite happy with the arrangement of the paintings on the far wall, but he couldn't quite figure out why. When David came by tomorrow they would sort it out, he told himself.

He'd been selling David Steadman's work for the past year and each vividly rendered oil painting and pen-and-ink drawing had sold within weeks of being hung, no matter how much they continued to raise the price. David had been working hard to get enough canvases ready for this, his first show, and Cam was excited to be a part of it. He'd put the word out to all his contacts in the New York art community, even taking out a small ad in a local art magazine for the opening, which was only a few days away. He was sure that, if they could get the proper exposure, this opening could well set the as yet unknown but extraordinarily talented artist on his way.

Cam walked through the gallery to the adjoining frame shop, which also served as his office. He reached for the cup of coffee sitting amongst the clutter of papers, tools and partially assembled wooden frames on the counter and sipped at it absentmindedly. He made a face and set it down again. It was ice cold.

He glanced at his watch. It was nearly six o'clock, though on the early summer day the sun was still shining brightly outside the large storefront window of his shop. He'd finished the three frame jobs for Mrs. Bernstein and he'd done what he could in the gallery, so he decided to close up and head home.

He set the alarm system and locked the doors. Stepping back on the sidewalk, a sense of wonderment and gratitude at the success of his small gallery overtook him as it always did when he looked at the words painted in clean black lettering on his large picture window—*McNamee Fine Arts Gallery & Frame Shop*. He'd started the place two years before, when the space, only a few blocks from his apartment house, became available.

Though he had no particular artistic talent himself, he loved art and could spend days at a time lost in museums and galleries, swept up in the worlds created by the talent of others. He was very comfortable around the tools and supplies needed to build frames, having grown up with a father who was a carpenter with a large woodshop at the back of their house. His father had taught him to build cabinets and simple pieces of furniture, and had given him his first miter box and tenon saw at the age of ten.

Cam enjoyed the process of building the frames for the photographs and artwork people brought into his frame shop. He liked helping them select the proper wood and matting to set the work off to greatest advantage. He enjoyed working with his hands and he liked the autonomy of owning his own business.

Shoving his hands into his pants pockets, he headed down the block. Ethan should be home soon. Normally just the thought of Ethan made Cam smile. Since Ethan had moved in, Cam had never been happier.

Except for the past few days. Something was off. Though Ethan had assured him otherwise, Cam was pretty sure it had to do with the scene with the man who called himself Maestro. If he thought about it, and he'd been thinking a lot about it over the past few days, the first small barb of unease had pierced his consciousness when Ethan had mentioned the emails he'd been exchanging with Maestro.

Usually Ethan and Cam discussed the details of their email and phone exchanges with the Doms they agreed to meet at the BDSM clubs. They would offer each other advice and encouragement, and afterwards share the details of the scene, good and bad. True, the situation wasn't ideal—Cam sometimes wished Ethan was a true Dom, or that he himself was, so they would be enough for each other in every respect. But mostly he accepted things as they were, and had thought their arrangement a good compromise to keep the spark alive.

But something had happened this weekend. For the first time, the easy openness between them was somehow strained. Cam had tried several times to get past whatever it was Ethan was holding back, but Ethan would only smile and shake his head, assuring Cam there was nothing wrong.

Cam tried to shrug off the sense of foreboding he felt. They'd both known the risks of going into this kind of arrangement. When you played the intense, sensual games they indulged in at the clubs, emotions were bound to get entangled from time to time. Whatever had happened, he knew if he could just get Ethan to talk about it, they could work through it.

Cam could hear the sound of voices when he entered the apartment. It took him a second to realize it was the TV. When he entered the living room, he saw Ethan sitting on the sofa with a can of beer in his hand.

"Hey, what a nice surprise. I thought you'd be late because of the client thing in Staten Island."

"It didn't take as long as I thought so I managed to miss the worst of rush hour."

"Great. Maybe we can go out for Chinese or something. I don't feel like cooking tonight, do you?"

Without answering, Ethan stood, setting his can on the coffee table. Walking around the table, he held out his arms. As Cam moved into them, Ethan pulled him close and held him tight. Cam could sense the need in his embrace and the feeling of unease that had been hovering on the edges of his consciousness assailed him full force.

Gently he disengaged himself from Ethan's arms and stepped back, peering into Ethan's face. Instead of meeting his gaze, Ethan looked away, dropping back down onto the couch.

"Something's going on. What is it, Ethan? I can't stand this tiptoeing around we've been doing the last couple of days. Whatever's going on, you need to tell me. We need to talk."

"Yeah," Ethan agreed. "Yeah, we do."

"It's got to do with that guy, Maestro, doesn't it?" Cam asked, certain he was right, not sure suddenly he wanted to know. Whatever was going on, it couldn't be good, but it needed to be brought into the open before any more damage was done.

Ignoring the nervous feeling in the pit of his stomach, Cam sat down beside Ethan and took his hand. "Talk to me. I'm listening."

Ethan gazed into his face with those sparkling blue eyes and Cam's heart actually ached with love. Was it about to be broken?

"Oh, Cam—" Ethan squeezed Cam's hand back and his voice cracked. "I—I fucked up. I didn't mean to. It—it just happened."

Cam felt as if his blood had been drained and replaced by ice water. When he spoke, it was with a calmness he didn't feel. "It's okay, Ethan. Whatever it is. We can handle it together. Tell me."

Ethan began to tell him, haltingly at first, about the incredible connection he'd felt with Maestro, about how quickly and deeply he fell under the Dom's skillfully wrought, magical spell. "That's why I stopped the action. I was afraid of the intensity of the experience. It felt like...like cheating on you. I didn't want to do that. I don't want to do that."

Relief surged through Cam, even though he knew there was more to the story. At least they were talking about something real now. "Hey, it's okay. We knew going in that this kind of thing could happen. It's the nature of D/s—when it's done right, you can't help but have an intense reaction. I understand. I think you should have let him take you all the way. I mean, that's the point, isn't it? We can't make each other fly—why not let someone who has the skill and desire take you there? It doesn't have to lessen what you and I have."

Ethan looked sharply at Cam. "Are you saying you fly when you scene with your Doms? I didn't know that."

Cam shook his head, smiling at his jealous lover. "I tell you about my scenes, Ethan. You know from time to time I get lucky and meet someone like Maestro. Sir Anthony, for example. You remember him, right? Until he started pressing to meet outside the club, we shared some pretty intense scenes. You were cool with it, right? Why should this be any different?" Cam was sure there was more and though he was half afraid to hear it, he knew he must. "What's the rest of the story? You say you fucked up. Is there something else?"

"I saw him again," Ethan whispered, closing his eyes.

"You saw Maestro?" Cam was confused. They'd spent the rest of the weekend together. When would he have even had a chance to meet him? Then it clicked. "Today? You saw him today?"

"Yeah."

Cam's stomach twisted. "You spent the day with another man? You didn't go to the office? You didn't meet those clients in Staten Island?"

"No, no! Not the day. Just a little while. I met him for coffee at midday. Except we didn't make it to coffee."

Cam leaned back against the sofa and closed his eyes. "Go on," he said softly.

"Cam, I love you."

"I know. Go on. Tell me." Cam willed his mind to stay empty, shutting out the unwelcome images trying to push their way in.

Ethan expelled a rush of air. "Okay. I called him because—"

"*You* called *him*," Cam interrupted, Ethan's words hitting him like a slap in the face.

"Yeah." Ethan looked stricken. "I—I don't really exactly know why. I felt like maybe if I saw him again, you know, just as a regular guy, not in a scene, I could get some perspective. I was thinking about him too much. He was in my head and I couldn't focus on my work. So I called him and asked if he wanted to meet for coffee."

"For coffee."

"Yeah."

"But you...didn't make it."

"I picked him up at his office because I had the car. We started talking. You won't believe this twist, I knew the guy in high school in Jersey but I didn't realize it. He's changed a lot."

"You knew him?"

"Yeah, his name is Andrew. Back then he went by Andy. We hung in different crowds. I didn't really know him well, but apparently he had some kind of crush on me back then and he looked me up. Found me on Facebook because of that reunion thing."

"Whoa. Wait a minute. Are you saying he sought you out, knowing who you were? You didn't just connect because of the Dom/sub thing?" Cam liked this less and less.

"Yeah. He was really embarrassed to admit it. I mean, he should have told me right away and he knew it. He explained he didn't want me to associate the man he had become with the nerdy kid he used to be. He said he meant to tell me sooner, but one thing just led to another and he couldn't figure out how to work it in."

"Weird..."

"Yeah, but I'm okay with it. I mean, he's not like a stalker or anything. But that's not what's bothering me now. It's that... we, uh..."

Here we go, Cam thought, dread in his heart.

"We kissed."

Cam waited for more. When it wasn't forthcoming, he said, "Okay. You kissed. And then?" Cam was clenching his jaw and his fists. He forced his fingers to uncurl and parted his lips, waiting for the words that would crack his heart.

"Nothing. I took him back to his office building."

Cam stared at his lover, not sure he'd heard him correctly. "That's it? You made out in a parked car for a couple of minutes and then dropped him off? Are you sure you're telling me the whole story?"

Ethan looked acutely uncomfortable. "Yeah. I mean, I had to get to my appointment. Plus, I was really confused, you know? I mean, I broke my promise to you. I saw a Dom outside the club scene. I kissed him. I kissed another man."

Cam eyed his lover, not sure how to react. The thought of Ethan and another man kissing wasn't that big a deal, or it wouldn't have been, if that's all it was. But obviously there was a lot more at play here, and a lot more at stake.

A heaviness dropped over his heart, weighing him down. Forcing his way past it, he asserted, "You and me. We love each other. We've been making it work for nearly a year now. Yeah, I'll admit the club scene only goes so far. But what we have—it's so special. I've never felt like this for another guy, Ethan. Dom or sub or vanilla. Never.

"Damn it." He slammed his hand on the arm of the sofa. "So you kissed a guy. What's the big fucking deal? We can work through this. So you saw a Dom outside the club. Okay. You came home and told me. You didn't go off and fuck the guy. It was just a kiss, right? So we move on. Shit, when you think about what we do at the clubs, what the hell difference does a little kiss make? We're stronger than that. Our love is stronger than that. Isn't it?"

Instead of shouting a resounding, reaffirming *Yes*, Ethan ran his hands through his hair and sighed. "You know, my life experience is different than yours. I guess I'm a slow study." He laughed without mirth. "It took me so long to come out of the closet, I had a lot of catching up to do. I've only been exploring my submissive feelings and needs for a few years. I've never lived 24/7 with a Dom like you did."

"Which was not all it was cracked up to be, believe me," Cam interjected, helpless anger rising in him at the direction he was afraid Ethan was headed.

Ethan waved his hand. "Maybe not. But it's an experience I haven't had. I'm not saying I want to break up with you. I couldn't do that. I love you. I want you in my life. And until last Saturday, I thought we'd figured it out—come to a good compromise with the club scene. I thought it was enough for me. But being with Andrew, I don't know. I think I'm coming to the point where..."

"Where..." Cam prompted in a whisper.

"Where it's not enough."

Cam stared at Ethan, speechless. What was Ethan really saying? He said he loved Cam and then in nearly the same breath he said it wasn't enough.

I did this. I pushed him away. I pushed him into the arms of his new lover by coming up with this stupid idea for us to play at the clubs. Even as he thought this, he knew it wasn't true. He would have lost Ethan even sooner if he'd tried to keep him home. Ethan needed an active D/s element in his life. If Cam were honest, he needed it too. But the part-time games had been enough for him. It had been the perfect compromise for the two subs, or so he had thought. Obviously, he had been wrong.

"*I'm* not enough, you mean," Cam finally said. "This Maestro, this Andrew, is he enough?"

"No. No, that's *not* what I'm saying. I love you, Cam. The last thing I want is to lose you. But I realized something today. As much as I love you and what we share, these weekend play dates with virtual strangers just aren't enough anymore. It's like

Andrew opened some kind of gate inside me that I can't just push shut and ignore. The thing is, I don't know what the answer is. I don't know what to do about these feelings. I don't know how to incorporate D/s in our lives in an honest way without destroying our relationship in the process."

Cam closed his eyes while the world shifted and tilted beneath him. Was he going to lose this man to another? To a Dom, who could offer him the one thing Cam couldn't—the chance to truly submit, not just in play scenes, but for real, with the heart and mind, not just the body.

Because no matter how hot their sex life was, no matter how close their friendship, Cam could never be that for Ethan, just as Ethan couldn't be it for him. Maybe it had only been a matter of time before one or the other of them met a man so compelling, so masterful, that they were willing to chuck what they had to pursue that possible dream and make it a reality.

Cam stood. The oxygen in the room was suddenly insufficient. He couldn't seem to fill his lungs. "I—I need to get some air. I'm going to take a walk."

Ethan stood as well. "I'll go with you."

"No." Cam held out his hand, palm up. "I need to be alone. I'm sorry. I just need to be alone for a while." He turned abruptly, not wanting Ethan to see the tears that threatened to spill. "I won't be long."

Before Ethan could protest, Cam slipped out the door, closing it softly behind him.

chapter 5

ETHAN BECAME AWARE of the ticking of the old windup clock they kept on the mantle. He opened his eyes, for a moment completely disoriented. The room was dark, save for the city lights filtering through the windows. He was clutching his cell phone in his hand. He stared at it blankly for a while as he came fully awake.

He sat up, calling out, "Cam?" though he knew Cam wasn't there. The apartment felt empty—abandoned. He reached for the lamp and flicked it on. The time on the DVD player said 10:23 P.M.

After Cam left, Ethan had just sat there, stunned. Never before had Cam just walked out on him. They'd had disagreements before, even arguments, but never had either one just vacated the premises. But then, neither one had ever kissed another guy or admitted that it had mattered so much.

Had Ethan's mistake been in telling the truth? Should he have kept Andrew and the stolen kiss a secret? He knew even as these thoughts entered his mind that he couldn't have done that. Even if he never breathed a word and never saw or communicated with Andrew Townsend again, there was no going back to where he'd been before.

It had been scary to say aloud what had been churning in his brain for the last several days. *It was no longer enough.* He needed more in his life. While he loved Cam with all his heart, he could no longer deny the submissive yearnings Andrew had unwittingly unleashed in him. Nor, if he were completely honest, could he deny his attraction for the man himself.

But damn it, he hadn't handled it at all well with Cam. Cam wouldn't have been so brutally blunt, as he had been. Cam would have been able to explain himself better, to convey his feelings without coming across like a confused, selfish jerk. Cam would have found a way to couch his words with gentleness and love.

That's because Cam was the kindest, most thoughtful man Ethan knew.

And he had hurt that man. The look of anguish that slid over his face when Ethan said those words…*it's no longer enough…* cut Ethan to the quick. What had he been thinking, to put his own selfish need for D/s over his love for Cameron McNamee, the best thing to ever happen to him?

Ten minutes passed, then twenty, then an hour and still Ethan sat, his mind alternating from numb emptiness to agonized ruminations on how he could have handled the conversation better. He thought about going out to find Cam, but where would he go? Cam loved to roam the city and by now he could be anywhere. In fact, if Ethan left the apartment, Cam might well return while he was gone.

He fished his phone from his pocket and called Cam. The phone went directly to voicemail. Ethan listened to Cam's silky, sexy tenor and then said, "Cam, please come home. I need you."

Then, inexplicably, he must have fallen asleep. Now he flicked open the phone again and called Cam for a second time. Again it went to voicemail and Ethan began to worry, not only that Cam was ignoring his calls, but that something might be wrong. He'd been gone for nearly four hours.

Quickly Ethan used the toilet and washed his face. Grabbing his keys, he hurried out of the apartment, bounding down the four flights of stairs to the lobby. He stepped outside, looking up and down the boulevard.

He began to walk with no particular plan in mind when suddenly it occurred to him where Cam might be. Picking up his pace, he made quick work of the three blocks to Cam's gallery. He peered in the window. The gallery itself was dark, but he could see a light on in Cam's workshop behind it. Using the key Cam had given him for emergencies, he unlocked the door, mentally reviewing the alarm code in case it was set.

The alarm pad just inside the front door indicated that the alarm was not set, confirming Ethan's suspicion that Cam was in the back room. "Cam?" he called out, as he moved toward the workshop. "It's me. Are you okay?"

He poked his head into the cluttered room. Cam was leaning over the desk, his head cradled in his arms, his hair obscuring his face. Ethan moved closer, his heart surging with affection for the sleeping man.

Lightly he touched Cam's shoulder. "Cam? You okay?"

Cam opened his eyes and sat up abruptly. "Oh. I must have fallen asleep. What time is it?" He yawned.

"Nearly eleven. I was worried when you hadn't come home and didn't answer your phone."

"My phone?" Cam patted his jeans pocket and frowned. "Huh. Where the heck is my phone?" He began to rummage in the pile of papers spilling over his desk. "Oops. Here it is. I must have left it here this afternoon." He peered at it. "Dead as a doornail." He shrugged sheepishly. "Sorry about that."

"Hey, it's okay." Ethan smiled. Cam was forever forgetting to charge his phone. He also frequently misplaced it, along with his keys and his wallet. "I'm just glad you're okay." After a beat, he added, "*Are* you okay?"

Cam stood and stretched, a strip of flat, firm stomach showing beneath his T-shirt when he lifted his arms. "Yeah. I'm sorry, Ethan. I'm sorry for just bailing on you. I just...I just needed some time to think."

"I love you, Cam. Whatever else is going on, please know that. I don't want to lose you."

Cam nodded and looked down, shoving his hands deep into his jeans pockets. "I love you, too." He looked up again, his eyes sad. "But that kiss—it' didn't just happen. I mean, you called him, you arranged to meet him."

"Cam, I'm really so—"

Cam raised his hand. "No, I'm not asking for an apology, Ethan. I'm not. I'm glad you were able to tell me. We've always agreed never to keep secrets from each other. But we have to think this through. What it means for us. What we want it to mean."

"What we want it to mean?" Ethan was confused.

"Yeah. Is this the first crack in the seam of our relationship? Do we define it as a mistake you made and move on? Or do we look at what got you to that point. What's missing in your life that drew you to this other man."

"Oh, Cam, please, there's nothing missing. You're all I want." Ethan pleaded, hating the pain he saw in Cam's green eyes.

"Maybe," Cam said softly. "But I don't think I'm all that you *need*."

Ethan was quiet, taking this in. In his heart of hearts, he knew Cam was right. He needed more than the weekend play dates with dominant men in contrived public scenes. He longed for the chance to submit in a meaningful way to someone who mattered to him. But he loved Cam, damn it!

Cam touched his arm. As if listening in on his thoughts, he offered, "Look, we don't have to fix this right now. It's late and we're both tired. I shouldn't have walked out on you like that. It was childish and I apologize. We'll work this through. We will. Let's just let it be for now, okay? The main thing we agree on is we don't want to fuck up what we have between us. We'll figure it out."

"Yeah," Ethan replied, praying Cam was right. Cam reached for Ethan and Ethan stepped into his arms, nuzzling against Cam's neck. He moved his hands over Cam's strong back, slipping his hands beneath his T-shirt to stroke his warm skin. He could have stood there forever, breathing in Cam's scent and holding him close.

Cam was the first to pull away, unwinding Ethan's arms from around him. "You hungry? I'm starving."

Ethan realized that he was, too. "Yeah, I totally forgot dinner. Wanna stop for some pizza before we go home?"

They picked up a pie at their favorite local pizza joint and walked back toward their apartment building, each lost in his own thoughts. Andrew had inserted himself back into Ethan's mind. True, they'd only shared a stolen kiss, but it could have been more—much more, and he knew it.

Andrew had suggested Ethan cancel his appointment and come back with Andrew to his apartment to continue their "talk."

Ethan, who had felt that kiss from the tips of his ears all the way down to his toes, well knew what would end up happening if he went home with Andrew. And while his cock kept whispering, "Do it, do it," he listened to his heart instead.

Back at their apartment, Cam and Ethan sat at their kitchen table. Cam served them each a slice of pizza on a paper plate while Ethan removed two cans of beer from the fridge. It felt good, just sharing a simple meal.

After they'd eaten, they moved to the bedroom, neither bothering to turn on the light. The room was bathed in the glow of city lights from the window. Ethan watched Cam getting undressed, admiring his tight ass and strong, lithe physique. Cam slipped off his underwear and stretched out on their bed, his thick cock at half-mast.

"I just realized I forgot to have dessert," Ethan said, licking his lips.

Cam offered him a lazy smile. "I shouldn't have lain down. I'm too wiped even to get up and brush my teeth."

"That's okay. You just lie there. Don't mind me." Quickly Ethan shucked off his own clothing, save for a pair of black bikini briefs that hugged the rising erection beneath them. Dropping onto the bed beside Cam, he fell greedily on Cam's cock, inhaling his earthy, masculine scent as he licked a circle over the fat helmet of his shaft.

"Hey, cut it out," Cam protested weakly, though his cock hardened beneath Ethan's lips. Ethan gripped the base of Cam's shaft, capturing it between thumb and forefinger and forcing it upward. Cam groaned and let his arm fall over his face.

Ethan lowered himself over Cam, taking him deep, letting the head slip back into his throat. He sucked and licked the warm, smooth flesh while stroking Cam's balls with his other hand. Cam moaned with pleasure.

After a few minutes, Ethan pulled back, letting Cam's rock-hard cock fall from his lips. "Hey," Cam protested. "Don't stop."

"Oh, but you're so tired," Ethan teased. "I'm keeping you up."

"You got me up," Cam laughed. "Now you better get me off."

Ethan smacked playfully at Cam's erect shaft. "Oh yeah? Is that an order, Sir?"

"Yeah. On your knees, slave boy. Worship my cock."

Ethan put his hand in his underwear, stroking his own shaft. He had a sudden, urgent need to be inside Cam. To lay claim to him with his cock. "I have a better idea," he murmured. Kicking off his underwear, he reached for the lubricant and smeared some over the head of his cock.

Reaching for Cam, he pulled him back into his own body so they were cradled like spoons. "I need to fuck you, Cam. I have to." Cam didn't answer, but he pushed his ass back toward Ethan's groin in silent agreement.

Ethan positioned himself, pressing the head of his lubed cock against Cam's tight little hole. Grabbing Cam's hip, he guided himself inside, relishing the hot grip of muscle massaging his cock.

"Ah," Cam cried, the sound part pleasure, part pain. Ethan he knew was moving too fast, but he couldn't help it. He was driven, desperate to be inside Cam, to stake his claim, to find an outlet for his passion.

"Sorry," he murmured against Cam's ear, forcing himself to slow down. Reaching around Cam's body, he found Cam's cock, still rigid and slick from Ethan's earlier attention. Closing his fingers around it, he pulled up, drawing a gasp of pleasure from Cam's lips. While he moved inside his lover, he stroked the rigid shaft until Cam's shallow, rapid breathing and trembling body made it clear he was on the edge.

Ethan began to thrust hard, his balls slapping against Cam's ass, his fingers flying over Cam's shaft. "Now," Ethan urged with a groan, as he released his seed deep inside the velvet clench of Cam's body. He felt the hot, sweet gush of Cam's ejaculate over his fingers and lifted his hand to his lips to taste the salty-sweet cum.

They lay still for several moments, hearts pumping in unison. Ethan, hovering on the edge of consciousness, realized his cock had slipped from Cam's ass. Summoning the last bit of his strength, he reached for the box of tissue, gently wiping between Cam's cheeks before cleaning himself.

He lay on his back and reached for Cam, who hadn't moved. Gently, he pressed a palm flat against Cam's back, loving the feel of his skin. He assumed Cam had fallen asleep, and he was about to reach for the sheets to cover his lover, when Cam, still turned away, spoke.

"Maybe I should meet this guy."

"What?"

Cam rolled onto his back and turned to look at Ethan. "Maestro. Andrew. We both agree we don't want him coming between us, but the fact is, he exists. You could decide to never see him again. To put him behind you and move on for the sake of our relationship. But I'm not sure that's the best thing. He'd always be there, hidden away maybe, but never really gone."

Cam turned his body toward Ethan and draped a leg over Ethan's stomach, resting his head on Ethan's chest. Ethan brought his arm around him and stroked his silky curls, loving him so much his heart hurt.

Cam continued. "We know we love each other. There's no question there. But this guy's had an impact on you. He's a real Dom, which we both know is pretty damn rare. Yeah, my gut reaction when you said you'd kissed him was to be hurt, to feel betrayed. But at the same time, I can understand it. We're not joined at the hip. The very nature of the D/s games we play at these clubs leaves us open to something like this happening. Maybe there's a way..."

Cam stopped, pausing for so long that Ethan, wildly curious where he was going with this, prompted, "a way..."

He lifted his head and smiled at Ethan. "I don't know. I don't really know what I'm saying at this point. I'm so tired my eyes are crossing. But let's think it over. Maybe just having Andrew and me meet could ease some of the tension you're feeling. Put everything right out there on the table. What do you think?"

Ethan pondered the idea for a while. It did make a kind of sense. He did want to see Andrew again, to scene with him again, he couldn't deny it. But not at the cost of fucking things up with Cam. Maybe Cam was right—by introducing the two of them, he'd be eliminating the "sneaking around" aspect of it all, which had troubled him from the beginning.

"I think it's a good idea. I'm not sure what he'll think about it though."

"I guess," Cam offered, "there's just one way to find out."

chapter 6

"ANDREW? THERE'S A call for you." Vivian, Andrew's assistant, called from the outer room. "Want me to take a message?"

"Who is it?"

"Said his name was Wise. Ethan Wise. I didn't recognize the name so I didn't put him through directly."

Andrew's heart lurched into a rapid thumping. He hoped he sounded calmer than he felt. "Okay. Thanks. I'll take the call."

Andrew had spent the last twenty or so hours doing his level best to put Ethan out of his head. The kissed they'd shared in Ethan's car the afternoon before had turned his insides to molten lava. It had taken every ounce of self-control not to beg Ethan to reconsider his refusal to come with him to his apartment. He knew Ethan had been turned on by the kiss. The flush on his cheeks, the look in his eyes, not to mention the bulge in his jeans were testament to that. Andrew's cock had throbbed in response, his lips, his tongue, his entire body aching for more.

But bruised pride, as well as respect for Ethan's wishes, had kept him silent. When Ethan had dropped him back at his office, he'd figured that was it—Ethan would again return to being only a fantasy, only this time he would fantasize for the real man Ethan had become, the longing all the more acute now that he knew what he was missing.

The phone rang and Andrew stared at it for a second, almost afraid to lift the receiver. Mentally he chided himself to get a grip. He was the Dom, after all, the one supposedly in control. "Andrew Townsend."

"Andrew. Hi, it's Ethan."

"A nice surprise."

Ethan laughed. "Yeah, sorry to call your office line, but your cell phone was going directly to voicemail and I wasn't sure if you'd get the message."

Andrew patted his jacket pocket and found it was empty. Confused for a moment, he remembered he'd slipped it into his briefcase on the subway, along with some papers he was looking at when the train had pulled to his stop. "I'm sorry. I didn't realize I didn't have it handy. I'm glad you had the idea of calling my office." He paused, adding casually, "So, what's up?" *Besides my cock.*

"I was wondering if you could meet for lunch or a drink or something. Just to talk. I wanted to discuss something with you and I'd rather do it in person."

Just to talk. Well, talking was better than nothing. Andrew looked at his watch. "Sure, let's do lunch."

They agreed on a Thai place Ethan liked that was midway between their offices. Andrew was very curious about just what Ethan wanted to talk about, but decided to wait and see what he came up with. After he hung up the phone, he leaned back in his chair, swiveling it toward the window. He smiled, putting his hands behind his head. Twice now Ethan had basically walked out on him—first by ending the scene prematurely, and then by sending him away after that one perfect kiss.

Andrew touched his lips at the memory and shook his head. Ethan kept walking out, but then he kept coming back. Andrew couldn't help but grasp at a glimmer of hope for something more than unrequited lust. Maybe, just maybe, Ethan wanted more than he was letting on.

Fueled by this idea, Andrew tried to return to his work but found he couldn't concentrate on a thing. He opened his email and handled a few work-related responses. He had an hour until they were to meet. He estimated it would take about twenty minutes to walk to the restaurant.

He turned back to his computer, again making a futile effort to focus. After a few minutes he gave up, pushing away from the desk with an exasperated sigh. Closing his programs, he stood and reached for his suit jacket, thought better of it and left it hanging. He retrieved his cell phone from his briefcase and pocketed it in his trousers.

As he passed Vivian, he said, "I've got an appointment and then a lunch meeting. I'll be back in a few hours. Call if you need me. I have my cell."

Andrew removed his tie on the way down in the elevator, recalling Ethan's casual attire the day before. He walked for several blocks, stopping to window-shop from time to time, mainly just working off his nervous energy by moving. The day was warm and he was glad he'd left his jacket behind. He unbuttoned several of the buttons on his shirt and slowed his pace to cool himself off.

He arrived at the restaurant ten minutes early but went in anyway, figuring he'd get them a table and menus before Ethan made his appearance. In the dim light he could see the place was long and narrow, the walls painted a pale teal and hung with wooden masks that Andrew assumed must be Thai. Delicious smells of chili pepper and spiced oil and coconut wafted to his nostrils.

Looking toward the tables, he saw Ethan's white-blond head bent over a menu and he grinned, pleased to see Ethan was as eager, or at least as prompt, as he was. Ethan chose that moment to look up and their eyes locked. Ethan rose and smiled as Andrew headed toward the table.

They shook hands, as if they hadn't ever kissed, as if Ethan hadn't been nearly naked and subjected to Andrew's flogger, the connection as intimate as any sex. Andrew slid into the booth across from Ethan. Ethan was wearing a royal blue soft cotton button-down shirt that set off the brilliant light blue of his eyes. The bulge of his biceps pulled the fabric taut over his arms. Andrew realized he was staring and looked down, picking up the large red menu and flipping it open.

"What's good here?"

"Everything. I really like the ginger chicken. If you like it spicy, the beef with black bean curd and red pepper is really good."

"I like it spicy, all right," Andrew quipped, unable to resist. He was pleased to see the slight flush creep over Ethan's cheeks.

The waiter took their orders and left, returning a moment later with two steaming cups of jasmine tea. Andrew leaned forward, cupping the ceramic mug between his palms. "So, what is it you wanted to discuss?"

"Cam. Cameron McNamee, the guy I live with."

"What about him?"

"He wants to meet you."

Whatever he had imagined, this wasn't it. Andrew raised his eyebrows. "He does?"

"Yeah. I—I told him about the kiss. And about the strong connection I felt with you, right from the beginning. He's a really cool guy. He's sub too, as you know, but, even though he's younger, he's had a lot more direct experience in the scene than I have. He lived as a 24/7 collared slave for a while with a guy. He's been aware of his sexual kink since he was sixteen-years-old. Me, on the other hand," Ethan shrugged, looking embarrassed. "I was in such denial for so long about everything to do with my sexuality that I've had some catching up to do."

"Okay," Andrew said slowly. "And Cam's wanting to meet me affects this how?"

"Well, he knows how much it means to me—to connect with someone who really gets it." Warmth suffused Andrew at this comment, but he kept his face impassive, still not sure where this was going. "And he wants to be a part of that. I mean, to meet the person who affected me that way. He's—" Ethan paused, a look of pure bliss settling over his features. "He's really a pretty amazing guy."

Pain shot through Andrew's gut at this declaration, though at the same time he found himself moved by the sincerity and sweetness of it. "You really love him, huh?" he asked softly.

"Yeah." Ethan nodded. Then his face darkened. "But something's missing. I mean as far as D/s goes. We thought it would be enough—the club scene and all that but, for me anyway, it's too much of a game. I want more. I *need* more." Ethan's hand was resting on the table. As he spoke, he balled the napkin beside it into his fist.

Andrew reached impulsively across the table, putting his hand over the fist until Ethan relaxed his grip, his fingers easing.

"I know what you need, Ethan. I wish I could be the one to give it to you."

An image flashed in his mind, so vivid it superseded reality for a moment, blurring the real Ethan. The Ethan in his mind's eye was naked and chained with his back to a stone wall, his arms high overhead, his ankles in iron cuffs, his cock stiffly erect at his groin. He was sweating, the hair matted on his forehead, his face twisted in orgasmic pleasure or pain—it made no difference, because it was Andrew who was causing the reaction, Andrew who knew just how to push a submissive to very edge of his sensual envelope and then, with the slightest puff of breath, send him flying...

The waiter appeared with a laden tray, distracting Andrew from his daydream. Both men picked up their chopsticks and began to eat, saying nothing for a while as they concentrated on the delicious food.

"In a way," Ethan finally said, "I wish you could, too." He tossed his head as if rejecting the idea, and offered a sheepish grin. "I know how that must sound. One second I say I'm in love with Cam, the next second that I want to submit to you. I know I can't have it both ways."

"Can't you?" The thought leaped fully formed into Andrew's brain. He tried to dislodge it as impractical and impossible, but it remained firmly entrenched.

"What do you mean?" Ethan looked at him curiously.

"One Dom, two subs. Why not?" Andrew bit his lip, aware even as he said the words aloud that they were crazy. Not to mention, he had no wish to share Ethan with another. He wanted him all to himself. One sub was plenty, if that one sub was Ethan Wise.

Ethan threw back his head and laughed. "That's a good one. Shit, a relationship is hard enough between two. Imagine the complications of adding another person."

Andrew forced a laugh in return. Ethan was right, anyway. What the hell had he been thinking? Not admitting the seriousness of his offer, he tossed out, "I was just talking about a scene. You know, the three of us at a club or whatever."

Ethan sobered and nodded. "I thought of that. We've always gone to separate clubs, mainly because of me. I get jealous when Cam is with someone else. I don't think Cam has a jealous bone in his body."

"Well, I can understand jealous feelings when you think of someone you love with another person," Andrew said. "But if you were both submitting to the same guy, it would be different. You remained connected as subs. I imagine it could even intensify your feeling of union because you're doing it together."

"I never really looked at it that way," Ethan nodded thoughtfully.

The glimmer of hope Andrew had felt earlier bloomed into a small, bright light inside him. He tried to ignore it. He'd planted the seed, now he'd just have to wait and see if it germinated. Meanwhile, he added, "So, anyway. I'm cool with meeting Cam. How about Friday?"

Ethan shook his head. "Friday's no good. I have an overnight business trip in Philly. I won't even make it home until midnight. It sucks because Cam has an opening at his gallery that night. I wanted to be there to support him."

"He has his own gallery? Where is it located?"

"In Hunter's Point. It's on 48th Street, off Jackson Avenue. He's built it up from nothing in just a couple of years. A real labor of love."

Andrew consulted his mental calendar. He had thought to go by the Lair on Saturday night, but knew he'd rather spend the evening with Ethan, even if it did mean adding his lover into the mix. "How about Saturday then? We could meet for dinner."

"That would be perfect." Ethan reached over the table and squeezed Andrew's arm. Andrew closed his eyes a moment, forcing away the electric thrill Ethan's touch wrought in him.

Nothing more pathetic, he thought, *than a fool in love.*

~*~

"David, look," Cam said excitedly. "That's Nancy Harris." Nancy Harris was an art critic who wrote for *New York Magazine*. She was known for her usually scathing reviews and was very difficult to please. Cam didn't mention this part, however. "Wow, I didn't expect her here tonight. Just the fact she showed up at all is a major coup for us."

David Steadman, a short, prematurely balding man in his early twenties, bounced nervously on his toes, speaking in a rapid, nervous patter. "Oh my god, oh my god. Look! She's coming over here. Do you know her? Will you introduce me? Do you think she likes my work? Oh, shit, she's writing something on a pad. She hates it. She hates the whole show. The west wall's hung all wrong. I told you we shouldn't have placed those paintings together."

Cam laughed and put his hand on David's arm. "Relax, David. It's fine. We've got a great turnout for a new artist and I've already sold nearly a third of the paintings. Take a deep breath and smile. I've met Nancy a few times and despite reports to the contrary, she doesn't bite. I'll introduce you."

Once David and the art critic were introduced and talking, Cam moved toward the refreshment table to see if he needed to open another bottle of wine. Happiness bubbled through him at the success of this opening. With the economy tanking as it had been lately, sales were markedly off and he'd worried David's work wouldn't get the attention it deserved. He really was an extraordinary talent just waiting to be discovered. It could well be that this was his night and Cam was proud to be a part of it.

If only Ethan could have been there. Cam looked around his gallery at the twenty or so people milling about the room, when his eye was caught by a very tall, broad-shouldered man with short dark hair, a prominent nose and a strong jaw. Standing in profile to Cam, the man was examining the painting hung closest to the door. He was dressed in a black shirt and black denim jeans and even from where he stood, Cam could see the character in his face.

Such a striking man was surely taken, and probably by a woman. From where he was standing, Cam couldn't see the man's hands, not that a wedding ring or the lack of one necessarily meant anything. Cam caught himself up short. *What the hell?* Why was he checking out this guy like he was a potential lover?

The man chose that moment to turn his head, staring straight at Cam. Their eyes locked for a long, intense moment during which Cam forgot to breathe. There was something compelling in his gaze. Cam was frozen to the spot, powerless to look away. He could feel the beginnings of an erection and his mouth had gone dry.

"You've outdone yourself with this one, McNamee." Cam was wrenched from the man's gaze by Jordan Haber, an amateur art critic who roamed the city, adding his own very original take on cultural events. He was flamboyantly gay, with heavy eye makeup and more piercings than Cam could count, but his online blog actually carried quite a bit of influence in certain circles of the artistic community.

Cam turned to Jordan, who tonight was dressed in a torn black tank top spattered with paint and white leather pants that molded perfectly to his long, thin legs. Long, pointed-toe cowboy boots of bright red completed the ensemble. "Thanks, Jordan. David's work is selling itself. All I had to do was hang it."

They began to talk about the show, and who was there and who wasn't. While Jordan was holding forth about another gallery opening he'd been to earlier that day, Cam looked back to the door to see what the tall, handsome stranger was doing.

He wasn't there.

Cam scanned the room, searching for the man amidst the crowd, but he had gone. With a sigh, Cam turned back toward Jordan, pretending to listen to whatever he was saying, his mind's eye filled with the vision of the tall, sexy man with the brooding look. Cam resisted a sudden, absurd impulse to run out of the gallery and see if he could spot the guy on the street.

Which was ridiculous, of course. Even if the man had come properly into the gallery, there to view the show, what would Cam have said? "Hi, you're incredibly sexy. Would you like to fuck me?"

He knew his feelings were wrong on so many levels. First of all, he was completely and totally committed to Ethan. Second, he didn't even know if the guy was gay, though by the look they'd exchanged, he was now willing to bet he was. And finally, he knew nothing about the man. For all he knew, he could be a serial killer. So, he was hot—seriously hot. So what? Ethan, Cam firmly told himself, was hotter. End of story. Feeling resolute, Cam turned back to his guests, determined to forget the sexy mystery man.

~*~

"I've heard of this place," Cam said, when the taxi let them off in front of Sushi Fusion, the latest trendy, and, as far as Ethan knew, very expensive Japanese restaurant. Andrew had chosen the place, insisting that the dinner be his treat. "Andrew must have some clout—I've heard it takes a month just to get a reservation here, unless you know someone."

Ethan grinned, trying to ignore the butterflies smashing their fluttery wings against his insides at the thought of Cam and Andrew meeting. "Maybe the owner is one of Andrew's sub boys," he said lightly.

They entered the restaurant and were greeted by a Japanese woman dressed in a traditional silk kimono with a powdered-white face and lacquered red lips. "You are, please?"

"We're meeting someone here. Andrew Townsend."

The woman scanned a small clipboard and tilted her head in a nod. "Yes, please. He is here. Follow me, please."

They followed her past a fountain that tumbled into a pond filled with darting silver and orange fish, through a large dining room, most of the tables of which were filled. She stopped in front of a rice paper sliding door and tapped lightly against its wooden frame.

"Shoes off, please," she said, pointing to their feet. While the men complied, she pushed the door open and announced, "Your guests, Mr. Townsend."

"Arigato, Yukiyo-san." Just the sound of Andrew's deep voice sent tingles through Ethan's spine. He gestured Cam ahead of him and they stepped up into the small room. Cam stopped suddenly just inside the door, causing Ethan to bump heavily into him.

"Cam? You okay?" Ethan stepped beside him, confused and concerned. Cam was staring point blank at Andrew.

Andrew unfolded his long limbs from a low polished wood table that rested on the tatami mat flooring. His head nearly brushed the low-hanging paper lantern as he stood. Cam continued to stare, open-mouthed.

Ethan was embarrassed at his lover's strange behavior, but didn't know what to do about it. "Andrew Townsend, meet Cam McNamee." Stepping around the table, Andrew moved forward and held out his hand to Cam. This common gesture seemed to snap Cam out of whatever peculiar trance he'd fallen into.

Taking Andrew's hand, Cam swallowed and laughed nervously. "I've—I've seen you before, haven't I?" It occurred to Ethan that Cam might have indeed seen Andrew before, in the guise of Maestro at one of the BDSM clubs. Maybe he'd even scened with him!

Before he could suggest this, Andrew spoke. "Yes. I apologize I didn't introduce myself last night. I'm not even sure why I stopped by. I guess I was curious to see the man who has stolen Ethan's heart so completely."

"Last night? What?" Ethan interjected, now utterly confused.

"I came by Cam's gallery last night." Andrew explained, while at the same time Cam burst out with, "*He's* Andrew? I can't believe that's Andrew. Now I get it, Ethan. I totally get it." Cam turned to Ethan with shining eyes. Ethan wasn't quite sure what was going on, nor quite sure what to think.

"Wait, I don't understand. You've already met? What's going on?"

"Let's sit down and straighten this out," Andrew said smoothly, moving back toward the table, which had several plump cushions set around it. Andrew was looking at Cam, a faint, enigmatic smile on his face. Ethan followed his gaze and saw the erection clearly outlined beneath Cam's thin linen trousers and the penny finally dropped.

"You get it, huh?" Ethan murmured as they sat side by side across from the Dom, not entirely sure whether to be glad or jealous. He was, he decided, a little of both.

chapter 7

As if they'd been waiting just outside the door, two more women, also dressed in brightly colored silk kimonos, glided into the small room, each carrying a tray. The first one set a small sake bottle with a tiny porcelain cup over its top in front of each man. The second placed a large ceramic mug beside each bottle and poured hot green tea.

They slipped out of the room in a rustle of silk and smiles, only to return almost at once with a tray of beautifully arranged sushi on a huge rectangular black ceramic plate, flanked by small mounds of coral-colored ginger and pale green wasabi.

"Wow," Cam enthused. "That looks almost too pretty to eat."

"I hope you don't mind," Andrew said. "I took the liberty of ordering ahead for us. If you don't care for sushi, this will be followed by a shrimp and vegetable tempura and various Japanese noodle dishes."

"Are you kidding? Not care for sushi? It's the food of the gods." Ethan reached for a piece of sushi with his chopsticks and popped it into his mouth. He closed his eyes as he chewed, the expression of sheer joy on his face making both Andrew and Cam smile. Andrew couldn't help the small jolt of jealousy at the way Cam and Ethan leaned in toward each other, as if each were a flower and the other his sun.

Cam helped himself to a piece of sushi, carefully smearing a bit of wasabi over its top and adding a sliver of ginger. Ethan looked admiringly around the room and asked, "So how did you get in here? Cam's heard it's nearly impossible to get a reservation unless you make it a month in advance, and even then, to get this fancy private room, how'd you manage that?"

Andrew smiled and shrugged. "The owner is a friend of mine. You might have come across him in your nocturnal travels. He goes by the name Samurai in the club scene."

Cam, who had been sipping from his cup of sake, nearly spit his drink out. "Samurai? No way. Doesn't he own Red Dragon down in the Village?"

Andrew nodded, amused at Cam's reaction. Red Dragon was a BDSM dungeon for hard-core players and admittance was by invitation only. "Co-owner, yeah. With his slave, Gordon."

"Small world," Ethan mused.

They spent the next half hour eating the deliciously prepared sushi and cooked dishes, their sake bottles replaced several times by bowing, smiling Japanese women. As if by silent agreement, none of the three brought up the real reason they were there. Andrew still wasn't entirely sure what the real reason was.

Ethan had been fairly nebulous about why he wanted Andrew and Cam to meet. Was it to prove to Andrew how committed Ethan was to his lover, or to give Cam a chance to see Andrew was no threat to their relationship? Or did he have some kind of ménage action in mind—a scene at the club perhaps, as Andrew had suggested.

It had been a whim to stop by Cam's gallery. For some reason that night, instead of heading to one of his favorite haunts, he'd stayed on the subway, changing to the train that would carry him from Manhattan to Brooklyn. He was familiar enough with the streets to find 48th and Jackson, and Cam's was the only art gallery on the block, set between a florist's shop and a dry cleaners.

His conscious thought was that he'd scope out the competition—see just who was keeping him from claiming Ethan for his own. He had thought this would give him an advantage when they actually met the next night.

He'd recognized Cam at once from the photo on Ethan's Facebook. Cam was very easy on the eyes, no question about that, with his auburn hair hanging in unruly curls about an open, sunny face with slanting green eyes and a ready smile. He was wearing a rumpled white linen jacket over a green silk shirt that clung to his broad chest like a second skin.

Andrew hadn't been prepared for the instant connection between them when their eyes had met. It was a kind of recognition, though he was sure he'd never seen Cam before—he would have remembered. For the first time since he'd begun to email Ethan several weeks before, someone besides Ethan had slipped into Andrew's dreams.

Until that moment, he'd had some vague idea of domming both guys, but the intent behind it was really to get at Ethan, to keep him in his life on some level, even if it were only superficial playing at the club. He'd figured Cam would be part of the package deal he had to buy to get what he really wanted.

He hadn't counted on his reaction to Cam, which manifested itself not only as a sudden, raging hard-on, but also by the too-rapid beating of his heart and a heat that licked along his face and throat as if he were standing beside a roaring bonfire.

He'd seized the moment when Cam was distracted by someone to make his escape, sure if he stayed, he'd end up making a fool of himself and ruining his chances with either guy by coming on too strong.

He was more relaxed now, calling the shots, watching the two sexy subs as they enjoyed the meal. He decided to sit back and see what page the lovers were on. He wanted them both, of that much he was certain.

Over sweet rice cakes and green tea ice cream, Ethan brought the subject Andrew was sure was on all their minds to the fore. "So, Cam and I have been talking. He understands my need for a more authentic submissive experience. To tell you the truth, we aren't really sure what to do about it, but he thought at least by meeting you, it would put a face to whatever's going on between us."

"Yeah." Cam nodded his agreement. "I've been wondering something all night, though."

"What's that?" Andrew inquired.

"I've been in the New York D/s club scene for several years now. I thought I knew every Dom out there, every Dom of any consequence that is. How come I never ran into you?"

Andrew shrugged. "I'm fairly new to it, myself. I only moved to the city from New Jersey last year, when I took a new position in an electrical engineering firm here. As to the club scene, I enjoy it, as far as it goes, but I don't spend every night hanging out at them. I prefer something more…intimate." He couldn't help but shift his gaze to Ethan as he said this. "Or as you said, authentic."

Cam looked uncomfortable and Andrew had the feeling he wanted to talk to Ethan in private. Andrew was dying to suggest a scene with the two handsome subs, but still couldn't get much of a feel of their interest level. Deciding to put it out there and see what happened, he said, "I have a proposal, but I don't want you to answer right away. After I've made it, I'm going to step out for a while and find Samurai to thank him for the incredible service and food. You two can talk over my idea and we can discuss it when I come back, okay?"

Both guys nodded. Andrew took a breath and launched in. "I'm not going to lie to either of you. When Ethan and I met at the club, I was completely taken with him. I was secretly plotting in my head how to steal him away from the man who waited at home for him." He nodded toward Cam, who didn't respond, except to place his hand proprietarily on Ethan's arm.

"Then I met you, Cam," Andrew continued in the silence. "Just seeing you at the gallery—I don't know if you felt it too, but something passed between us. I don't know. It was as if..." He paused, trying to come up with the words.

"As if we'd met before," Cam said softly. "As if we'd already been lovers." There was a strange light in his emerald green eyes and Andrew found he couldn't look away. This time it was Ethan who draped his arm lightly over Cam's shoulders, pulling him close.

What the fuck am I doing? Andrew found himself thinking. *I want them both but all I'm doing is making each one jealous of the other. This is a crazy setup. I should end this before it starts. Before I get in too deep.*

He ignored his own advice, plunging on. "I was thinking, if the two of you were game. I'd like to try a scene with you both at the same time. I'll respect all preset limits, of course. The only thing I would ask is I don't want to do it at a club. I don't want the public aspect, where we're performing for an audience of gawking guys. I want it to be real. We can figure out the details on the limits and all that if you guys are interested."

Ethan started to say something but Andrew held up his hand. "No. Please. Don't say anything yet. I want the two of you to have a chance to discuss this without me around. Believe me, I understand and respect the fact you're committed lovers. I don't want to do anything that might jeopardize your relationship with each other. By the same token, I have to tell you, I'm so drawn to the both of you. It's more than just a sexual attraction. It's almost as if I was..." He trailed off, embarrassed at how hackneyed what he'd been about to say was.

This time it was Ethan who supplied the missing words. "...born to this."

"Yes," Andrew admitted, unable to keep the intensity out of his tone. "Yes."

~*~

Once Andrew had left, neither of them spoke for a moment. Cam felt lightheaded. He wasn't sure how much of this was due to the several bottles of sake he'd consumed and how much to the strangeness of the situation in which he found himself.

When he'd first suggested Andrew and he meet, he'd thought it would be a way to diffuse Ethan's obvious intense reaction to the guy. By bringing the three of them together in one room, with all their cards on the table, he would essentially stake his claim on Ethan, while trying to keep an open mind for whatever kind of D/s arrangement the two of them wanted to work out.

He hadn't expected the fierce, almost violent pull of desire he'd felt at seeing the tall stranger at the door of his gallery.

Though no words had passed between them, the naked longing transmitted by their glance had frightened Cam. To discover it was Andrew, the very man who had wrested this same response from Ethan, was something he was still trying to grapple with.

There was something about Andrew, some kind of subliminal communication between Dom and sub that spoke to both Ethan and himself. It was a connection even more immediate and intense than he'd felt for Bryan, the man who had kept him collared and in chains for nearly six weeks.

Theirs had been a brief and tumultuous affair, based on complete obedience on Cam's part, and heavy torture and nearly constant sexual attention on Bryan's part. He kept Cam on fire with lust nearly twenty-four hours out of the day. Cam was rarely allowed to come, but he was teased to erection nearly constantly, when he wasn't being milked, whipped, bound, gagged, caned, paddled or tied down and fucked. He slept on a pallet on the floor beside Bryan's bed, and was almost never invited up into his Master's arms.

He'd only been twenty-two at the time, fifteen years younger than Bryan, who had chosen Cam out of an eager group of sub boys who had auditioned to be his slave by answering an ad he'd posted on a BDSM personals site and spending a night with him in his dungeon. Bryan was handsome, extremely self-confident and very wealthy. He informed Cam that he'd been selected over thirteen other candidates and Cam had been young and foolish enough to feel pleased and impressed by this claim.

Cam certainly hadn't meant to fall for Ethan, another sub boy. Yet as he thought about it, their connection had been as immediate and certain as the one he now found himself feeling for Andrew, and which Ethan also felt. Did this mean something?

Was there such a thing as destiny when it came to matters of the heart?

He looked at Ethan, who was watching him, his head cocked to the side. "So, what do you think?" Ethan asked.

Cam didn't answer, instead leaning toward Ethan to kiss his cheek. Ethan turned his head so their lips met instead. As it always did, Ethan's kiss made Cam forget everything else. He lost himself in Ethan's touch, in the scent of his skin, in the taste of his kiss and the hot press of his lips.

They fell back after a few moments and Ethan reached over to pour Cam more tea from the pot the ladies had left behind. Cam was moved by this sweet, simple gesture. "I love you, Ethan. You know that, right?"

Ethan nodded. "I love you, too." A small furrow appeared between his eyebrows. "And I really don't want anything we do with Andrew to fuck that up. Yeah, I want a real submissive experience, but first and foremost, I want our relationship to remain intact."

Cam nodded, closing his eyes. The sake was making him sleepy.

The door slid open and Andrew stepped in. "Samurai sends his best wishes and this bottle of plum brandy. I couldn't talk him out of it." He folded his long legs beneath the low table and set the bottle and three tiny glasses on the table.

Cam was tempted to decline, too much alcohol already woozing its way through his blood, but the glasses were so small, he figured what the hell. Andrew poured them each some. Cam sipped at the strong, sweet brandy.

Andrew cocked an eyebrow. "So…"

Ethan spoke. "We haven't really made up our minds." Cam glanced at him, realizing this was true. They'd talked around it but never come out and said they'd do the scene.

Cam saw the flicker of disappointment in Andrew's eyes before he managed a smile. "Of course. You take all the time you need. I'm not going anywhere. Why don't you give me a call tomorrow sometime? We can talk it over then."

The ease that had pervaded the evening had evaporated. They finished their brandy and stood. Cam noticed no bill had been produced but assumed Andrew must have taken care of it when he went to pay his respects to the owner. He wondered if they should offer to contribute but decided it would make things even more awkward, as clearly Andrew was running this show.

Once outside the restaurant, Ethan turned to Andrew. "We had a great time. Thanks for the incredible meal. We definitely owe you one."

"Don't worry, I'll exact it in trade." Andrew laughed, his eyes glittering. He hugged each of them in turn. Cam liked the feel of his body, hard and lean, strong arms pulling him close and letting go too soon. He felt almost guilty for his attraction, until he recalled this was the man Ethan had kissed.

At that moment he understood they were standing on the edge of something big—something that would either propel their relationship to a new level of intimacy, or lay the groundwork for its destruction. The question was, did they step back and let it go, always wondering what might have been? Or did they take each other's hand, close their eyes and make the leap?

chapter 8

ANDREW STOOD INSIDE the door of his dungeon, imagining Ethan and Cam there, naked and kneeling before him. His prewar apartment was large, not only by New York City standards, but by any reckoning, with large, high-ceilinged rooms and three full-sized bedrooms. In a stroke of luck, when he'd accepted the new job, he'd taken over the lease from another engineer in his firm who was retiring and moving to Florida, and he'd been able to get the same rent-controlled deal. While still a lot more than he'd been paying in Jersey, he'd fallen in love with the space at first sight, and since his other expenses were fairly modest and his salary good, he'd been able to swing it.

He'd turned one of the spare bedrooms into a private dungeon, though he'd yet to entertain too many guys in it. He was, he knew, too choosy for his own good. While it had kept him from getting involved with guys he knew from the start weren't right for him, it had also left him pretty lonely over the years.

Nevertheless, he'd continued to outfit the dungeon, spending his spare time making diabolical instruments of torture he saw for sale online, but doing it for a fraction of the cost. He'd turned what had used to be a sewing room into a small workshop. Handy with tools, he'd constructed a simple X cross with sturdy hooks for wrist and ankle cuffs. Beside it sat a spanking bench he'd built using a steel frame and diamond plate aluminum legs on which he'd placed thick, black cotton cushions. The legs cranked apart using an oversized hand wheel. The center portion had a cushioned leather pad against which the slave's torso rested.

His favorite and latest device was the cock and ball stocks. It consisted of two four-inch by four-inch upright posts that were about three feet high and set about three and a half feet apart. Each upright post had forty-five degree supports to ensure the posts were stable and secure. A crosspiece of solid oak between the two upright posts formed the stock portion of the device. In the center of the crosspiece was a removable section that contained half of the hole through which the slave's balls were secured with a locking clamp. The cock fit over the top of the cross piece and was then secured with a steel u-bolt, which was tightened with butterfly wing nuts. He'd added wrist locks at the tops of the upright posts and ankle locks at the bottom.

Along one wall, he'd hung the usual assortment of floggers, whips, paddles and crops. In addition, he had a nice collection of cock and ball torture devices, along with rope, chain, gags and blindfolds, all stored neatly in an old-fashioned bureau tucked discreetly in a corner.

Last night he'd been disappointed to find Ethan and Cam hadn't yet made a decision regarding their private scene, but he'd understood and once he'd had time to cool down, he knew it had been wrong to press them so quickly for a decision. Better to let them sleep on it. As much as he wanted them both, he knew it wouldn't work if either one of them felt pressured into anything.

He'd tried to put them out of his mind the next morning, showering and dressing as usual, planning to work out at his gym before the day became too warm, but while he was lacing up his sneakers, his cell phone had rung. It was Ethan, a little out of breath, saying they'd discussed it and agreed they'd like to try a private scene.

Trying very hard to be cool, Andrew said, "That's terrific. When were you thinking?"

He expected Ethan to pick a day the following weekend, and was pleasantly surprised when Ethan gave a nervous laugh and offered, "We were thinking maybe now? I mean, today? If you weren't busy. I'm just thinking," he went on in a rush, "you know, now that we've decided and all, it would be better just to find out. You know, if it's right for the three of us. Speaking for myself, I honestly don't know if I could concentrate on anything if we had to wait another week."

"And this is good for Cam, too?"

A fraction of a second's pause and then, "Yeah. We're both up for it if you are."

"Great. Come on over then. We can discuss limits when you get here and go from there."

He gave them his address and they said their good-byes. Andrew had been planning to shower after his workout, but now he was planning a workout of a different kind. Excitement whipped through him as he stripped off his gym clothes, showered, shaved and dressed to receive his guests.

He was pulling on his boots when the intercom buzzer sounded. Hurrying to his front door, Andrew pressed the button. "Yes?"

"Hi, we're here."

"Come on up. I'll buzz you in."

In a few minutes there was a knock at his door. He opened it and ushered them in. They both wore blue jeans and T-shirts, Ethan's a light blue that offset his brilliant eyes and Cam's black, a slight tear at the neckline that made Andrew want to rip it farther to reveal his chest. His cock hardened at the thought, and at the proximity of the two handsome men.

They exchanged greetings and small talk for a few moments. He gestured toward the pair of matching dark brown leather couches he'd bought at an estate sale some years before. Ethan and Cam sat side by side on one of them, both looking endearingly nervous. "Can I get you something? A cold drink?"

Both shook their heads. He sat down across from them and leaned back, hoping to put them at ease. "I'm glad you guys are here. I really should apologize for last night. It was insensitive to ask for a response right away."

Ethan leaned forward. "No, it's okay. We had time to talk about it." He glanced toward Cam, who was looking down at his lap. "We—we both agree it'd be hot. Fun."

Andrew wanted more than fun, but he kept this thought at bay. Just having them here, agreeing to something more than just a club scene, was in itself a big accomplishment. He was a little bothered by Cam's seeming reluctance, though, and decided to face it head on.

"Cam? Talk to me. How do you feel about this? If this is going to work, we all need to be honest, brutally honest, with each other. Are you sure you're comfortable with this? It's not too late to back out. Absolutely no hard feelings. I understand you're a couple first. I don't want to do anything to mess that up."

Liar. If he could, he'd steal Ethan away. As sexy and hot as Cam was, Ethan had been the one to occupy his fantasies for so long. Ethan was the one he wanted. The thoughts flitted through his brain before he had time to censor them. He looked away, afraid his expression might have somehow betrayed him.

"Ethan didn't twist my arm on this," Came said. He looked at his lover and squeezed his thigh. "I think it'll be fun. Something different. We're both onboard."

"Okay." Andrew nodded, deciding to accept this at face value. "Then let's get a few ground rules established. Once you cross the threshold of my dungeon—"

"Your dungeon!" Ethan exclaimed, his eyes lighting up.

Andrew smiled. "That's right, my dungeon. It's fully equipped and even includes ball gags for boys who speak without being spoken to." Ethan flushed and looked down, which pleased Andrew.

He continued. "As I was saying, once you cross that threshold, and for the duration of the scene, you belong to me. What that means is, you don't speak unless spoken to. You answer any question directly and with complete honesty. You obey every command without hesitation. If you have a strong objection to something, ask to speak and then tell me why. I'll listen. I may still require that you do it, but I'll take your concerns into account. You with me so far?"

"Yes, Sir," Ethan and Cam said in unison. Then they looked at each other and smiled.

Andrew smiled too, forcing himself to work past the small, sharp stab of jealousy at the couple's closeness. "I believe in listening to my sub, to really paying attention to your reactions and cues, not just your words. I'm pretty good at gauging what you can take and when you need me to ease off, but in case I get it wrong, there's always your safeword. Ethan, I remember yours is football." Ethan nodded. "And yours, Cam?"

"Liver," Cam said.

"That's an unusual safeword," Andrew said.

"Cam hates liver," Ethan said with a grin.

"Understatement," Cam added. "When I was a kid, my misguided parents used to make me sit at the dinner table until I'd cleaned my plate. One time my mom made liver and I ended up sitting there for hours, covering it with ketchup, sugar, whatever I could think of to make it more palatable. They finally gave in and let me leave the table when it was time for bed. She never made liver again, at least."

Andrew nodded and smiled, though the story made him sad. "Okay. Liver it is." He surveyed the two of them. "I've never done a three-way scene. This is new for me, too, so we'll all be playing it by ear. Just remember, I'll be the one running the show. You'll be my slave boys. My subs. My personal sluts, understood?"

"Um," Ethan ventured.

"Yes?"

"About that. About sex…"

Andrew forced away the image of Ethan, naked and on his knees, spreading his ass cheeks for Andrew and begging him to fuck him. He'd already decided there would be no actual sex this first time out, even if both guys were begging for it. "I meant slut in a generic sense, that is, someone who is completely willing to do whatever I want. As far as sex goes, for the first scene I think we'll hold off. That's something you boys would have to earn." He understood the sub mentality—the moment he took the decision away from them, informing them there would be no sex, they would fixate on it and do their best to manipulate the situation to that end.

"We agreed no anal," Cam said.

"But oral would be okay," Ethan added.

"Not today, slave boy." Andrew suppressed a grin at the eagerness in Ethan's tone. He was definitely more into this than Cam. Andrew decided he would focus at first on Cam, to try and win him over. If the only way to Ethan was through Cam, then so be it. His cock actually ached at the thought of Ethan sliding his lips along the shaft, while Cam knelt beside him, eagerly licking Andrew's balls.

"I reserve the right to touch you. To stroke you, to feel your skin, to handle your cock and balls if it pleases me, to bind you, gag you and whip, paddle, crop, spank and cane you. I won't be using any anal toys on you, not today. That's more intimate than we're ready for at this point. You are not to come, no matter what. Unless, of course, I change my mind."

Neither sub spoke. Cam was looking down at his lap, on which his hands were twisting. Ethan was watching Andrew with that special light shining from his eyes. It was a light Andrew had seen dozens of times before that shone from subs' eyes when they were falling under his dominant spell. Ethan, at least, definitely wanted this.

Andrew stood and pushed his fingers through his hair, keeping his raging lust tightly under control. "Want to see the dungeon?" Both of them stood and Andrew led them along a narrow hall toward the room at the end. He stopped in front of the door and turned to them.

"No sub enters this room wearing clothing, unless it's something I've chosen for you. If you want to come in here, you need to strip."

"Right here in the hall?" Cam said, looking around as if someone might appear.

"It's private here, Cam." Andrew stepped close to Cam and put his hand on his chin, gently forcing him to look up. He stared into those lovely green eyes, silently exerting his will over the sub. He noted with satisfaction the softening of Cam's features and the beginning of a submissive shine in his eyes. Taking a chance, he dropped his other hand to Cam's crotch, thrilled to feel Cam's cock hardening beneath the denim.

Andrew spoke with a soft voice, but put the steel of his jaw behind it. "Do you have a problem with stripping for me?"

"Uh, no." Cam bit his lip. Andrew let his chin go, resisting the impulse to lean down and kiss him roughly on the mouth. Ethan had already pulled his T-shirt over his head and was kicking off his shoes. Andrew grinned at his eagerness, his mouth watering at the thought of seeing that beautiful naked body again, this time with no codpiece to hide his sex.

Andrew turned his attention back to Cam. If Cam balked, Andrew would call it off. Though he wanted them both something fierce, it had to be mutual on all their parts. He folded his arms and waited, holding his breath. Cam's eyes were on his face. Slowly, he reached for the hem of his T-shirt.

~*~

Andrew opened the door and gestured for the two of them to enter ahead of him. Ethan and Cam stood together, taking in the room. "Whoa, Andrew," Ethan enthused. "This is some serious equipment."

Andrew nodded, though he narrowed his eyes as he turned them on Ethan. "It is. I'll give you a little tour. But first, a reminder. Once inside the dungeon, you don't speak unless spoken to. You will address me as Sir. Is that understood?"

"Yes, Sir." Ethan looked down, his face heating. Cam reached for his hand, giving it a small, reassuring squeeze. Ethan flashed him a grateful glance. Andrew moved to stand directly in front of them. "Ethan, arms behind your back—hold your wrists, stand at ease. Cam, you too."

Cam dropped Ethan's hand and shifted to obey. Ethan's cock was hard and getting harder under Andrew's scrutiny. He hadn't been completely naked with another man since he and Cam had hooked up, nor, as far as he knew, had Cam.

When told to strip, Cam had hesitated in the hall and for a second Ethan had been afraid he'd changed his mind. It had been strange and even thrilling in a way, to watch Andrew exert his dominance over Cam, catching him with that fiery gaze and effectively willing him to obey.

They stood together, vulnerable in their nudity while Andrew remained fully clothed. He was wearing a black tank top that emphasized his broad shoulders. His pants were black denim, cut close along his powerful legs and on his feet were the same square-toe boots he'd worn at the club.

Without warning, Andrew reached toward them both, gripping each by the throat. Ethan stiffened and gasped at the sudden gesture, his heart at once tripling its tempo. Andrew's hold on his throat wasn't hard enough to choke, but certainly firm enough to get his complete attention. As always happened when someone gripped his throat in such a blatantly dominant way, Ethan's cock engorged and lengthened, his breath quickening.

He stole a sidelong glance at Cam, whose cock was also perking, though not yet at full erection. Cam's eyes were fixed on Andrew's face, his hands still dutifully clasped behind him. Ethan returned his gaze to Andrew as well. Andrew's eyes flickered from face to face, a fire lit from within.

"Slow your breathing, Ethan," he said, his voice low and seductive. Ethan drew in a breath, keenly aware of the strong fingers still wrapped around his throat. He tried to let it out slowly. "Good. Again. Slow, even breathing. Both of you."

After a moment, Andrew released them and stepped back. "That's good. That's what I like to see. Calm, obedient sub boys, cocks hard, paying attention." He left them standing in the center of the room and moved toward the corner that contained an X cross and two other contraptions.

Putting his hand on the second one, Andrew said, "This is the spanking bench. If we continue beyond today, you'll both become intimately acquainted with it, as I'm very fond of spanking my sub boys and I don't like them squirming around when I do it. Ethan, come over here and position yourself on the bench and I'll show you how it works."

Ethan moved toward it, unable to resist a glance at Cam, hoping Cam was still okay with all this. While it was true that in the end it was Cam who had insisted they give this private scene a try, Ethan knew in his heart of hearts Cam was doing it for him, or at least that was the primary motivator. Cam had been perfectly happy before—Ethan was the one rocking their little boat. He only prayed he didn't end up sinking it in the process.

Still, he couldn't deny he was incredibly turned on at the moment, thrilled to be back in a scene with the sexy Andrew. He knelt on the leg rests, easing his body over the padded body rest and reaching for the handles at its base to hold himself steady.

"That's right. You've used one of these before, I can see," Andrew said. "I can strap you down for especially intense sessions but for now, you just hold on." Once Ethan was settled, Andrew said, "This one has an added bonus." He gripped the large wheel on the side of one of the legs and as he turned it, they began to open. "I can crank these quite far apart, giving me better access to your body. It's quite subduing to be spread like this, completely at my mercy, wouldn't you agree, slave boy?"

Ethan legs were forced wider, his asshole, cock and balls completely exposed. A sudden sharp smack on his left cheek made him gasp, not so much from pain but because he hadn't been expecting it.

"A direct question, Ethan, requires a direct answer."

"Yes, Sir," Ethan breathed.

Andrew delivered two more smacks, one to each cheek and Ethan moaned, the blood tingling just beneath the skin. He closed his eyes, eager, even desperate, for the feel of Andrew's hard palm against his skin. Instead, he heard Andrew say, "I'm really proud of this one. It's a cock and ball stockade."

Ethan opened his eyes. From his position, he could see the wooden structure and as Andrew said what it was, he took in its delicious implications at once. He started to get up from the bench but Andrew's voice stopped him. "Did I tell you to move? Stay in position. Cam, you come here and I'll demonstrate this device. You should be honored to know you're the first person to actually try it out since I built it."

"Thank you, Sir," Cam said in a subdued tone. Ethan noted Cam's cock, though not fully erect, was getting there.

Andrew moved in front of Cam and reached for his shaft. Gripping it, he pulled it up, his fingers sliding over the skin Ethan knew was silky-smooth. A stab of jealousy pierced Ethan as he watched Andrew handle his lover in such an intimate way, but at the same time it turned him on. Cam's cock hardened, thickening and growing like a live thing beneath Andrew's skillful fingers.

With his other hand, Andrew gripped Cam's balls, squeezing until Cam winced, a small gasp coming from his lips. "Open your eyes," Andrew ordered. "Look at me." Ethan watched as Cam opened his eyes, staring up into Andrew's face while Andrew gripped his genitals. They stayed that way for several long seconds. Ethan could almost feel the erotic current passing between them. Cam was getting hooked, that much was clear.

Apparently satisfied, Andrew released Cam's cock and balls and moved to the stocks. He lifted the center section to an open position. "Stand in front of this and put your balls right here." He stroked the hollowed-out half-circle in the polished wood. "Then lower the cross piece. This keeps your balls in place and exposed for torture and pleasure. Put your cock on the top and apply the clamp to keep it in place."

Cam approached the stocks and stepped up onto the raised platform at its base. Ethan watched, his own cock twitching at the thought of being confined like that. Andrew knelt beside the stocks and pulled the black Velcro cuffs that hung at the base of each upright post, securing Cam's ankles into them. Directing Cam to lift his arms, he did the same thing to his wrists at the top of each post.

Andrew stepped back, staring slowly from one to the other—Ethan still kneeling and spread wide on the spanking bench, Cam tethered by his wrists, ankles and genitals in the stocks. Andrew's hand dropped to his crotch and he massaged his cock over his pants. It was fully erect and clearly outlined in his tight jeans, long and thick, arcing toward the hip. Ethan had to swallow to keep from choking as he imagined worshipping that huge phallus.

"I think we'll start with a nice warm-up." Andrew turned away, heading toward the wall that contained the whips.

"You okay?" Ethan mouthed to Cam, who nodded, his green eyes blazing. He looked so fucking hot like that, his broad chest shown to advantage by his raised arms, the dark auburn hair curling in a V at his sternum. Small gold hoops glinted at his nipples, matching the one in his ear. Ethan let his gaze drop to Cam's cock and balls, which were sticking lewdly out of the stocks, engorged and fairly begging for attention. He would have loved to kneel in front of Cam and suck them until Cam creamed against his tongue.

Though he'd never been able to successfully dom Cam, or vice versa, he was surprised to admit that watching Cam submit to Andrew was nearly as thrilling as submitting himself. He only hoped Cam was feeling the same way because he wanted this to work. As much as he loved Cam, Ethan needed a Dom. If he were honest, it went beyond that. He wanted *Andrew*. He wanted him bad.

chapter 9

CAM FELT INCREDIBLY vulnerable, with his balls caught in the viselike grip of the stock, his cock jutting hard above them. He looked at Ethan to his right, kneeling with legs spread wide on the spanking bench. They'd never played at the same time with a Dom. Both understood the power of a scene, even when one wasn't especially attracted to the Dom in question, and had agreed in the past that sharing a Dom might lead to unfounded jealousies or misunderstanding.

But something about Andrew had short-circuited Cam's normal caution. He still couldn't quite put his finger on it, but there was an allure to Andrew, an attraction that went beyond the physical. It was a *knowing*, if that was the right word. It was as if Andrew knew Cam, maybe even better than he knew himself. The feeling was at once alarming and exciting.

Ironically, though Cam had been the one to encourage Ethan as they'd talked through Andrew's proposal, he found himself reluctant when they'd first entered Andrew's apartment. He'd experienced a moment's misgiving as he sat down beside his lover and listened to the Dom outline his expectations. There was the very real possibility he might end up losing Ethan to another man.

Everything in Ethan's body language, from his eyes fixed intently on Andrew's face to the bulge at his crotch, made it clear Ethan had no second thoughts about what they were doing.

It was a little late, Cam thought with an inward smile, to worry now about whether he'd made the right decision. He was locked into the stocks by his genitals, his wrists and ankles cuffed in place on the posts, his lover naked and spread beside him.

Cam couldn't deny that he had agreed to the shared scene not only to keep Ethan, but because he too felt a strong urge to experience what Andrew offered. He wanted to feel the heat that coppery fire in Andrew's eyes promised.

Andrew approached him first, holding a round paddle that resembled a ping pong paddle. It was covered in red leather. Andrew stood in front of Cam and pressed the paddle against the head of Cam's cock. He drew it upward and held it in front of Cam's face. He could see the smear of pre-cum on the leather.

Andrew saw it too. "Slut," he whispered, a small smile curling his lips. He pushed the paddle closer to Cam's face. "Lick it off." Cam stuck out his tongue, tasting his own lubricant.

Andrew stepped behind him and Cam tensed, readying himself for the paddle's bite. Instead he felt Andrew's hands, the palms pressed flat as he moved them over Cam's ass, back and thighs. His touch felt good and Cam began to relax, closing his eyes.

After a full minute of the sensual massage, Andrew stepped to the side so he was standing between Ethan and Cam, the red paddle in his hand. Cam missed the feel of those strong fingers easing his muscles, but by the same token, his skin tingled in anticipation of the paddle. He glanced toward Ethan, who was watching them with an intense expression.

"Eyes straight ahead," Andrew snapped and Cam obeyed.

When the paddle struck his ass he drew in a sharp breath, unprepared for how hard the blow was. While floggers and whips covered a wider area, the paddle concentrated its force, and its sting was formidable. Andrew struck him again, just as hard, on the other cheek. Cam jerked involuntarily against the wooden prison, his cock and balls straining in their confines.

The sound of the leather-covered wood slapping against skin resounded in the room, along with the rasping gasp of Cam's breathing. His heart was thumping in his ears and he gripped the posts and squeezed his eyes shut, trying to go with the flow of the pain but failing. It was too much, too fast. He was used to the Doms at the clubs, who usually erred on the side of caution, moving so slowly they sometimes nearly put him to sleep.

Andrew moved closer, so close Cam could smell his cologne. Cam turned his face toward Andrew, barely resisting an impulse to stick out his tongue and lick Andrew's throat.

Andrew reached down and closed his long, strong fingers over Cam's shaft, drawing a moan of pleasure from between the gasps of pain. He didn't stop the paddling. If anything, he hit him even harder, but suddenly it was much easier to take, with those fingers working their magic on his cock.

"Slow down," Andrew whispered. Cam could barely hear him over the blood beating in his ears. "Ease your breathing. Show us your grace." Somehow just the words had a soothing effect. Andrew's voice was deep and lulling, almost hypnotic. He continued to paddle Cam's ass and thighs, his fingers moving in slow, sure ecstasy over Cam's bound cock. His balls, compressed and exposed beneath the wooden crosspiece, ached for attention.

Cam's hands eased, his fingers loosening their tight grip on the wooden posts. He leaned back, letting his tethered wrists and ankles take his weight. The paddling continued, but he no longer tensed for each blow. His focus was on Andrew's left hand, on the thumb gliding over the slit of Cam's crown, forcing more pre-cum to the surface and using it to lubricate his strokes.

"Ah, Jesus," Cam whispered, aware by the tightening in his balls he was very close to orgasm. He couldn't move—he couldn't get away from the paddle or those fingers. "Andrew. Sir...please," Cam managed.

"What." The paddling and stroking continued in tandem.

Cam swallowed and tried to catch his breath. "Please. I'm going to...you have to..."

"Surely you're not about to come?"

"Yes. I am. Please..."

Andrew delivered an especially savage blow that caught Cam across both cheeks at once, slamming him forward into the stocks, which caused his balls to twist painfully in their confines. Whether or not that was the intended result, its net effect caused Cam's impending orgasm to recede, though his cock remained hard as steel beneath Andrew's relentless fingers.

Andrew lowered the paddle and dropped Cam's cock. Cam sagged against his restraints, aware he was sweating. His heart was pounding. His bangs were matted on his forehead and falling into his eyes. He shook back his hair and blew upward, trying to get it out of his eyes.

He'd nearly forgotten Ethan was beside him. Despite Andrew's earlier admonition to keep his eyes forward, he stole a sidelong glance at his lover. Ethan was resting his head on his arm, watching them from his kneeling position on the bench, his legs still spread wide. His lips were parted, his tongue appearing on the lower one, his eyes hot with lust. Cam couldn't see his cock, but he bet it was erect.

Andrew was in front of him. He pulled Cam's face forward and leaned down, his face close to Cam's. "You'll come only when I tell you, no matter what I do to you, understand?"

Cam took a breath. "Yes, Sir."

Andrew moved closer, gently pushing the hair from Cam's face. He traced the line of Cam's jaw with his finger, drawing it downward along Cam's neck. The intimate gesture sent an involuntary shudder through Cam's frame. He wanted Andrew to kiss him. He never wanted the Doms at the clubs to kiss him.

He closed his eyes, half expecting, and half fearing the press of Andrew's lips against his own, with Ethan not three feet away.

But Andrew didn't kiss him. Instead he walked away, returning a moment later with a whip that had one single, braided cord of leather dangling from its handle. With a flick of his wrist, Andrew made the tail fly and curl through the air with a whooshing hiss that made both Cam and Ethan flinch. Andrew moved toward Ethan, his smile cruel.

"Your turn," he said.

~*~

Andrew had chosen to scene with Cam first by design. Partly to draw Cam in and partly to save Ethan, the best, for last. He hadn't expected his own strong reaction to Cam, or Cam's extreme receptivity. It wasn't often he connected so immediately with a sub during a scene. It had happened with Ethan at the club, but he'd just assumed that was because of his longstanding and unrequited desire for the guy.

Andrew hadn't gone easy on Cam, curious how he'd handle a good paddling while his cock and balls were caught in the stocks. He'd been more than pleased to find Cam's shaft as hard as the wood it was trapped in. He could imagine a Prince Albert piercing on Cam's cock, a gold hoop to match the ones at his nipples.

It had been very tempting to give in to Cam's obvious and intense need to orgasm. His sweet, breathy pleading, the "please" left hanging for Andrew to interpret—*please stop or I'll come, please don't stop and let me come*—had gone straight from Cam's lips to Andrew's cock, which throbbed in response.

He'd stopped the paddling, not because Cam had taken enough—he could have handled plenty more, Andrew was certain—but because of his own nearly overwhelming urge to drop to his knees in front of the sub and suck that thick iron rod, not stopping until Cam begged for mercy.

If they had been lovers, he would have done just that.

But they weren't. This was just a scene. A game. Nothing more.

He focused his attention on Ethan, who was eying the whip with a priceless expression, part trepidation, part pure, unadulterated lust. It was a superior whip, made from braided black and red leather, perfectly balanced. It was his favorite signal whip, excellent for indoor play because it wasn't too long. It still gave the wonderful crack of a bullwhip, but was more easily controlled. It threw so sweetly, uncoiling like an extension of his hand, always finding its mark with deadly accuracy.

As much as he had enjoyed paddling and stroking Cam, now he turned his full attention to the blond god who waited, spread and obedient, on the spanking bench. He knelt in front of Ethan, looking deeply into his eyes.

He'd never seen eyes that color—a pure, pale blue flecked with bits of sparkling silver. Ethan stared back at him, his lips slowly parting and then closing again to form a single word.

"Sir."

"I want to use this signal whip on you. Can you take it, boy? Will you take it for me?"

"Yes, please, Sir."

The memory of that first night he'd seen Ethan again, bound to a cross, another man dancing around him, snapping a thin nylon single tail against Ethan's taut flesh, assailed his mind. Was Andrew just another in a series of Doms? Was he just using Andrew to get off? How far could Andrew hope to go, with Ethan's lover standing just beside them?

Refusing to permit this line of thought from distracting him further, Andrew stood and moved behind Ethan. Ethan was bent forward, holding the handles on either side of the pad against which his chest rested. Andrew placed the coiled whip on Ethan's back.

"Don't move. If it falls off, you'll be punished."

"Yes, Sir," Ethan whispered.

Andrew knelt behind him and reached for the cock and balls dangling between his spread legs. He massaged the heavy balls for a few moments before sliding his hand up along the erect shaft. As with Cam, the tip was gooey with Ethan's pre-cum. Andrew used his index finger to draw the lubricant down over Ethan's smooth cock. He could feel a vein pulsing beneath his finger and he traced its line.

Ethan shuddered and sighed. The whip shifted on his back, nearly falling, and Ethan stilled. Andrew used his other hand to grip Ethan's balls while he began to stroke his cock in earnest. In short order Ethan was trembling, his breath coming in ragged gasps. The guy really had very little self-control, Andrew thought with a smile. They would both need serious training if he were to take them on.

If he were to take them on...

Stop. Focus on the scene.

"Fuck." Ethan groaned. The whip slid precariously close to his side.

"What poor discipline," Andrew said, shaking his head. He felt Ethan's balls tighten beneath his fingers and knew a few more strokes would send him right over the edge. "You better stay still. That whip is about to—"

Before he could finish the sentence, a spasm roiled through Ethan's body and the whip fell with a clatter to the floor. Andrew let go of Ethan's cock and balls and stood. He glanced at Cam, who was watching them with narrowed eyes and a fierce expression, his cock sticking out straight as a ramrod in its wooden prison.

"Oh dear," Andrew said, his tone dripping with mock disappointment. "Now you'll have to be punished." Ethan was still trembling. Andrew put a hand on his back and knelt beside him, speaking low into his ear. "You didn't come, did you?"

"No…no, Sir."

"Lucky for you. If you had, your punishment would go that much worse for you." Andrew retrieved the whip and let it unfurl to its full four feet. He could feel both men's eyes boring holes through the whip.

Bull, snake and signal whips were not casual play toys, and Andrew had spent months learning to use them, first practicing on strips of paper hung on his wall, and Dixie cups perched on ledges, before ever trying them out on human flesh. He appreciated how dangerous they were, and not at all the same as using a belt, flogger or even a cane.

Along with the difficulty in mastering the whip came a rush of intoxicating power. It didn't take strength to wield a whip, but its energy was like electricity that arced back into the user. He'd learned the secret to how a whip worked was the taper from the thickness at the handle to the almost string-like cracker at the business end. All that beautiful, supple braided leather was merely designed to get the tip moving at incredible speed. It was the speed of the whip's end that did the work and produced that heart-stopping sound.

Andrew always thought, if there was one sound that epitomized BDSM, it was the crack of a whip. It exploded like a clap of thunder from the hand of a god, sending the snake of leather through the air with savage and sensuous intent.

Slipping the loop over his arm, he pulled back his wrist and flicked it lightly forward, causing the whip to crack, which in turn caused both subs to flinch. Ethan's gasp was audible. His eyes were wide, his whole demeanor filled with an almost palpable yearning. Andrew licked his lips and swallowed, trying to ignore the raging hard-on in his jeans.

"Permission to speak." Cam's pure tenor sounded beside Andrew, who was focused at that moment solely on Ethan.

Distracted, he turned to Cam. "Yes?"

"Forgive me if I'm overstepping, but a signal whip is pretty intense for our first time out."

"Cam," Ethan blurted. "It's okay. And it's our second time. My second time. He knows what he's doing."

Andrew turned to appraise Ethan, who blushed under his gaze. "Sorry, Sir. I didn't ask permission to speak."

"It's okay this time. And Cam, it's okay that you asked. We're new together, the three of us. We're feeling our way. I'm glad you spoke up if you're uncomfortable." He turned to Ethan. "What about you? I do know what I'm doing and I know—"

He bit his tongue, aware he'd been about to admit he'd spied on Ethan the night before they'd met, and watched how beautifully the man took a lashing. "…I know from our emails you're comfortable with this kind of whip."

"Yes, Sir," Ethan said, keeping his eyes on Andrew.

Andrew turned toward Cam. "I have an idea. Since you're so worried about Ethan's wellbeing, I'm going to let you participate in his punishment." He moved toward Cam, releasing his wrists and ankles from their cuffs. He lifted the crosspiece and watched while Cam stepped out of the apparatus and stood down from the platform.

"Here's what I want you to do, Cam. Kneel under the bench and suck Ethan's cock while I whip his ass. I'll be watching, so make it good."

He counted the seconds while Cam stood, not moving. If he refused, that was it. End of the scene, time to pack up and call it a day. Maybe the whole damn thing had been doomed from the start. One sub at a time was plenty to handle. Two subs who were also lovers—what the fuck had he been thinking?

But to his surprise and vast relief, Cam moved toward Ethan and knelt down, scooting along the floor beneath his spread legs. He positioned himself so he could reach Ethan's cock and balls and began to lick and suckle them, making Ethan groan with pleasure.

Andrew watched the two lovers for a moment, noting with satisfaction that Cam's cock, which had flagged during their exchange, was again erect in its nest of auburn curls. "Cam, drop your hands to your sides and take his cock as far into your throat as you can. Then don't move. Your only job is to make sure that cock doesn't come out of your mouth while I whip him. Got it? If it does, or if he comes, you'll be both be soundly punished. Understood?"

"Yes, Sir," Cam said, his voice muffled from his position beneath the spanking bench. Andrew watched while Cam maneuvered himself with open mouth until Ethan's long, thick shaft disappeared down his throat.

Satisfied, Andrew moved to the side of the bench and let the whip fall to its full length. He flicked it in the air, causing it to crack. Again both subs flinched and he smiled, the power and confidence returning to his step as he positioned himself.

"You'll count for me, Ethan. Ten lashes. Do I need to tie you down?"

"No, Sir." Ethan's voice was husky.

He snapped the whip and the tip landed across Ethan's left butt cheek, leaving a pale line that quickly turned to dark pink. "One!" Ethan cried. Shifting slightly, Andrew let the second lash mark his other cheek with a nearly identical welt. "Two!"

He snapped the whip again and again and each time the dutiful slave boy called out a number, though by eight he was gasping and panting so hard he could barely form the words. Cam, meanwhile, remained impaled on Ethan's cock, his own cock jutting from his groin. Ethan began to jerk spasmodically, which caused his cock to thrust up and down, though Cam did his best to hold on.

When Andrew let the tenth lash fall, instead of saying, "Ten," Ethan blurted, "Oh, fuck. Fuck," drawing the word out, his eyes squeezed shut and hands clenched hard on the spanking bench handles. Cam pulled back with a spluttering cough and Andrew realized what had happened.

With a clucking sound, he shook his head. "Oh, dear. What happened, Ethan?" he asked, though of course he knew.

Ethan was flushed and breathing hard, still bent and spread in position. "I—I came, Sir. I'm sorry. I didn't mean to."

"No, of course you didn't. And you, Cam, what happens now?"

"We're to be punished, Sir," Cam said in a low voice as he wiped a bit of semen from his cheek with the back of his hand.

Andrew's cock was so hard it threatened to burst through the denim. What he really wanted to do now was take them both to his bed for an extended session of lovemaking. But these weren't his lovers. They were partners who'd agreed to a private scene, and that was the sum total of the situation, whether he liked it or not.

And so he said, "That's right. If we play again, that is. For today, the scene is over. You've both had quite enough."

He took bitter comfort in the look of disappointment that flashed over each handsome face.

chapter 10

ONCE THE GUYS were dressed again and settled in the living room, Andrew brought them Cokes and sat on the sofa across from them. Ethan's ass was still smarting from the welts and he wanted to go look at them in the bathroom mirror. He honestly hadn't meant to come, but Cam's hot mouth, coupled with the searing sweetness of the lash, had undone the last vestiges of his self-control.

Ethan wanted to talk to Cam alone, not entirely sure how things had gone from his point of view. He had been embarrassed when Cam piped up about the signal whip, as if Ethan couldn't make his own decisions. It wasn't like Cam to step on his toes like that. Usually he was the laid back one in the relationship, letting things roll over him with a calm ease that made Ethan envious. This was a new side of Cam, one that Ethan had brought out by threatening the relationship.

"How're you guys doing? I want to take your pulse, I guess, before I let you go," Andrew said. He looked so good, his long legs stretched out, his cock still visibly erect at his crotch. Ethan wanted to scoot down between his thighs and pull those jeans to his knees. He wanted to cover his face with kisses of gratitude for the incredible whipping.

Was he falling in love with another man?

"Let's start with you, Cam, since this was our first time together. How'd you like those stocks?"

"Amazing," Cam replied, a dreamy look coming onto his face that Ethan knew well.

"Not half as amazing as you looked in them," Andrew replied.

Cam smiled and ducked his head. He wasn't being falsely modest. Cam was the most unassuming man Ethan had ever met, and it was part of his charm. He honestly didn't know how hot he was. Cam, though he appeared slight and slender when dressed, was very strong, his muscles sharply defined and beautifully shaped. His ass, in particular, was perfect, two round, firm globes of solid muscle with an adorable dimple just above each cheek.

Ethan squeezed Cam's thigh proprietarily and smiled at Andrew. "He looks pretty hot, all right."

"Yeah," Andrew agreed, a look of naked longing washing over his face so quickly Ethan thought he might have imagined it. "And how about you, Ethan? You handled the whipping well, except for your indiscretion there at the end." Ethan felt his face heat and this time it was Cam who offered a squeeze to his thigh.

They talked for a while about the scene and their reactions, all agreeing it had gone well, and was definitely more intense than the usual fare dished up at the clubs. Ethan wanted to meet again but didn't want to be the one to bring it up. He hoped Cam would be the one, because, even though Cam said he enjoyed the scene and its intensity, Ethan still couldn't get a good, solid read on his real reaction.

It was Andrew, however, who said, "I've got a busy week, but my Friday evening is open. If you two would like to continue where we left off, I do believe a punishment is in order for both my errant sub boys?" He spoke lightly, his tone almost offhand, but Ethan could sense the yearning beneath it. He wondered if Cam could, too.

He looked to Cam. "What do you think? Want to?" Ethan, too, kept his voice light and nonchalant.

Cam looked into his eyes and Ethan's heart caught for a second. Behind the love he saw pain, but as quickly as it flashed, it was gone. "You want to, Ethan?"

"Yeah," Ethan admitted softly.

Cam nodded. "Then so do I."

They didn't say much on the subway ride home. Even though he'd just come the hour before, Ethan's cock pressed uncomfortably in his jeans as he watched a replay of the sexy scene in Andrew's dungeon in his head. Cam was likewise lost in his own thoughts.

When they got off the train and were walking the block toward their apartment building, Ethan turned to Cam. "How was it? For real, now. Not what you think I want or don't want. Not a formal processing of the scene with the Dom. How was it for *you*—your gut reaction."

Cam didn't answer right away, but then Cam often took time to respond to questions. He liked to think the question through and give a measured response. Ethan had learned to wait. Finally Cam said, "It was very intense. I think now our decision not to scene together with the same Dom was a wise one. I was jealous and I was afraid for you. Afraid he was going too far, too fast. And then I felt stupid because obviously you guys had already negotiated that in your emails, though I didn't know it. I realize now we've never talked in that much detail about our club scenes. I realize that though I love you, I don't know you as well as I thought."

"Cam," Ethan said, feeling as if he'd been punched in the stomach.

Cam took his hand, his voice earnest. "No, please Ethan. I think you misunderstood me. That's not a reproach. It's not your fault. It's how we've set things up. We've kept that part of our lives separate from each other. I've been with you for nearly a year and I had no idea you could take a single tail whipping the way you did. It was very intense, being underneath you like I was, your cock down my throat. I could feel every bite of that whip reverberating through your body. It was incredible. I think…"

He paused for a long time before continuing. "…I think I want to try it again. I want to meet with Andrew again. He's not your average Dom, that's for sure." They stopped talking as they walked into their building and up the several flights of stairs to their floor.

Once inside, Cam resumed. "Listen, Ethan. I know how into this guy you are."

Ethan started to protest but Cam stopped him with two fingers to his lips. "Hush. Listen to me. Again, this isn't a criticism. I say it because I understand. I feel it too. In the brief time we've been with the guy, I feel more from him that I ever have with any Dom. More than with Bryan, even, and things with him were very intense, at least for a while."

They stood together in the center of the room and wrapped their arms around each other. Cam, being the shorter, rested his head on Ethan's shoulder. "The thing is, Ethan. I don't want to lose you. I don't want to lose *us*. We as a couple mean more to me than finding an authentic D/s experience."

"Me too," Ethan said, but as the words came from his mouth, he realized he wasn't entirely sure this was true. The thought was unsettling and he pushed it from his mind.

They moved together into the bedroom and by some silent accord began taking their clothes off. They lay down side by side on their bed. Ethan stroked Cam's firm stomach, pleased to note his rising cock at Ethan's touch. Cam reached for Ethan and they began to kiss. After a few minutes Cam pulled away. He nuzzled against Ethan's neck while he reached for his cock. "If I don't fuck you soon I'm going to explode."

Ethan laughed. "You wanna fuck me, huh? Not if I get to you, first." They began to tussle playfully. Though Ethan was easily the stronger of the two, Cam was more agile and it wasn't long before he had Ethan pinned beneath him.

Cam let out a triumphant whoop, punching a first into the air. That slight movement was all it took. Within a second, Ethan gained the advantage, flipping Cam over on his back, strong thighs pinning his shoulders to the mattress.

"Hey, no fair," Cam cried, struggling beneath him. Ethan leaned down, smothering Cam's words with his kiss. Cam quieted and they kissed again for several long moments. Ethan's cock collided with Cam's, one harder than the other. They pulled away from each other's mouth, licking, biting and stroking each other's flesh with a fierce hunger. They twisted their bodies until each found the other's cock.

Ethan closed his lips over the mushroom crown of Cam's cock, sighing against it as Cam's warm mouth did likewise to him. They began to undulate together, thrusting in rhythm. Cam was the first to pull away. "I gotta fuck you. Now." He reached for the lube and squirted some onto his cock. The urgency in Cam's voice made Ethan roll to his hands and knees. He touched his forehead and shoulders to the bed, his invitation clear.

Cam positioned himself behind Ethan and slid his cock between Ethan's cheeks, gliding it up and down until Ethan begged, "Do it, Cam. Fuck me. Please." Ethan sighed with pleasure as the head of Cam's cock nudged gently against his sphincter. He wriggled back, eager to feel its penetrating fullness. Cam moved slowly at first, giving his lover a chance to adjust to his girth. Ethan, impatient, pushed back, grunting at the slight pain of muscles not yet sufficiently relaxed, but wanting Cam too much to care.

Cam grabbed his hips and thrust hard. "That's what you need, isn't it," he whispered fiercely in Ethan's ear. Ethan groaned in reply, his cock like a bar of steel between his legs. He stroked himself in time to Cam's thrusting, supporting them both with his shoulders and forehead as Cam took him hard.

It wasn't long before Cam shuddered and stiffened, shooting his seed deep inside Ethan. Ethan fell forward against the bed, taking Cam with him. He rolled back and Cam fell away. Ethan grabbed a tissue and wiped perfunctorily at Cam's cock and tossed the tissue aside. Cam lay inert, his head lolling to the side, his eyes closed, a satisfied smile on his face.

"I'm not done with you," Ethan informed him, his cock nearly bursting. He pushed Cam's legs up toward his stomach, spreading them in the process and exposing Cam's tight, pink hole. Grabbing the lube, he squirted some directly onto Cam's nether entrance and crouched between his legs.

Cam opened his eyes when Ethan pushed the head of his cock between his splayed cheeks. "Tired," Cam murmured, his eyes fluttering shut.

"Don't care," Ethan grunted back. He pressed into Cam's perfect heat, groaning with pleasure as his cock was squeezed by the tight ring of muscle just inside. He pulled back, savoring the clench, forcing himself to go slow.

"Open your eyes," he ordered. For some reason, when he fucked Cam in this position, whatever dominance he possessed came to the fore. Cam opened his impossibly green eyes and focused them on Ethan's.

"Yes, *Sir*," he murmured with a small, saucy smile.

Ethan laughed in response, but couldn't help but wonder what Andrew would have done if he'd dared to use that insolent tone with him. With this, Andrew returned in full force to his thoughts and he slammed hard into Cam, pent up lust and desire making him reckless. Cam responded by thrusting his hips forward, taking Ethan in deep.

He kept his eyes locked on Cam's for as long as he could. When the pleasure became too great and the orgasm too close, he allowed his eyes to shut and his head to fall back. His balls tightened as a tremor shook its way through his body. He came hard, jerking in spasm after spasm of hot, aching release until there was nothing left.

Cam reached up and pulled Ethan down onto him, wrapping his strong arms around him. "I love you, Cameron McNamee," Ethan whispered.

"And I love you, Ethan Wise. Now let's talk about..." but Ethan didn't hear the rest, as sleep dragged him into its drowning embrace.

~*~

Ethan was naked, his wrists bound tightly with thin cords of white rope, his cock thrust forward, his balls hanging low, weighted with clover clamps on which Andrew had attached lead fishing weights.

Cam, also naked, knelt in front of Ethan, his wrists shackled behind his back. He was bobbing up and down on Ethan's shaft, which caused the clover clamps to sway.

"Stick your ass out, slave," Andrew commanded and Cam complied.

Andrew held a long rattan cane, which he whipped through the air, letting the rattan land on Ethan's chest, catching both nipples. Ethan cried out, "Thank you, Sir!"

"You're welcome." He struck Cam's pert little bottom next. Cam, his mouth full of cock, said, "Mwan myoo, herr."

Andrew struck him again."What's that? I can't understand you."

Cam pulled back, breathing hard, long enough to gasp, "Thank you, Sir!" Ethan's cock fell from his lips.

"Bad boy," Andrew said, reaching down and pulling him up by the hair. "You let Ethan's cock fall out of your mouth. Now you'll have to pay…"

Usually Andrew watched porn when he masturbated. He especially enjoyed *Bound Gods,* for which he actually had a paid subscription, but that afternoon, alone in his apartment after the guys had left, he found all he had to do was close his eyes and let the fantasies roll out before him in vivid Technicolor. He could see the dark pink welts blooming against Cam's fair skin and the ice blue of Ethan's eyes. He could hear the thwack of the cane and the sensual cries of his slave boys.

His balls tightened and he reached for Ethan's head, the imaginary Ethan, who was now kneeling obediently at Andrew's feet, his mouth open, his eyes closed. Gripping Ethan hard by the hair, he held him in position while he fucked his face. He pushed past the soft palate at the back of Ethan's mouth, lodging his cock in Ethan's throat. Ethan opened his eyes, his expression pleading and for one perverse moment Andrew considered holding him that way until he passed out.

His own lust won out, however, and he pulled back, pummeling Ethan's mouth in his fantasy, though in fact it was his own hand flying over his rigid shaft, moving harder and faster as he neared his climax. He came so hard his semen shot several feet in a series of volleys, landing in white blobs on the hardwood floor. If Ethan were there, he'd have him crawl to it and lick it up.

But Ethan wasn't there.

Ethan and Cam had gone home. The two lovers had shared a scene with him and then they'd been on their merry way. At least he'd extracted a promise of their return the next weekend, though he knew those plans could change.

With a sigh, Andrew heaved himself to his feet and pulled up his jeans and underwear. He passed through his bedroom and into his bathroom, turning on the hot water in the shower. He stripped naked and appraised himself a while in the bathroom mirror.

Here he was, thirty-three-years-old, his body firm, his cock in good working order, his mind sharp and his heart aching. He was successful in his career, but his love life sucked. He'd had serious relationships before, but invariably the thrill faded, usually sooner rather than later. He'd even lived with two different guys, though neither relationship had lasted more than a few months. One of them, Joseph, had been a sub he'd met at a club back in Jersey. Joseph had claimed he wanted to live the lifestyle 24/7. He begged Andrew to make him his fulltime slave boy and submissive and at first Andrew, twenty-nine at the time, thought he'd found his dream partner at last.

But when he'd tried to make it real for them, Joseph had resisted. At first Andrew thought he was just moving too fast for his less experienced lover, and he'd tried to tailor Joseph's training to meet his needs and desires. After a while, however, it became apparent that Joseph wasn't serious. He liked the BDSM games but balked at any real show of submission. He loved a good heavy flogging, for example, but was damned if he'd let Andrew tell him when or how to come.

The experience had been a sharp reminder that fantasy does not always equal reality, and just because someone claims to be submissive, doesn't mean they truly are. It wasn't that Joseph had set out to trick him—it was just that he played by different rules. To him, it was and always would be just a game.

How excited Andrew had been when Ethan had reappeared in his life, the fantasy boy now a real live man, gay and sexually submissive to boot. He hadn't counted on the complications Cam would present. Andrew couldn't deny the real pull of attraction he felt for Cam, though he was aware of Cam's resistance toward him, or maybe it was just Cam's possessiveness of Ethan.

Whatever the reason, the challenge of winning him over, along with Ethan, was all the stronger because of it. "I want them. I want to own them both," he said aloud to the mirror. But what were the chances of that? It was one thing to scene with two guys. It was quite another to possess them in the way he longed for.

"You don't even know them," he argued with himself, though he knew it was an argument he'd lose. Because he *did* know them. He knew them in the primal way Doms and subs who were born to connect knew one another. It was a carnal knowledge that was coded into their DNA. They were, quite literally, destined for one another, whether or not they chose to accept that destiny.

Andrew sighed and turned away from the mirror, stepping into the shower stall and pulling the glass door closed. He adjusted the water and leaned back into it, letting the spray splash over his upturned face.

As he washed his body, his analytical engineer's mind clicked into play and he asked himself, "What do you want out of this thing? Are you really prepared to take on two subs at once? Is such an arrangement wise? Wouldn't it be safer to find a guy who's not attached? A sub who wants you and only you?"

That's when he realized something dramatic had shifted in the way he approached his life. He didn't care if the arrangement was wise or safe or sensible. He was tired of always weighing the pros and cons of every damn thing he did or thought. He was sick of taking the path of least resistance in an effort to keep his shriveling heart intact.

Yeah, the odds were good that this thing, whatever it was that was developing between him and the two sexy sub boys, would either fizzle out or blow up in his face. For once, he didn't give a flying fuck. He wanted what he wanted. And damn it, he was going to get it.

chapter 11

"YOU ASLEEP?"

"No," Ethan answered. "Drifting. What's the matter?" Ethan was on his back, Cam curled into him in his favorite position, his head on Ethan's chest.

"Thinking," Cam answered. It was Wednesday night, or more accurately, very early Thursday morning. It had been a strange week so far, as he waffled in his mind about what he really wanted from this developing ménage. Ethan was so obviously smitten with this guy and Cam wasn't sure what to do about it. The intermittent flashes of jealous pain that had burned his psyche during their first scene and afterwards, had eased over the week. Or rather, they'd been offset by his own lingering lust for the sexy Dom.

Ethan had gone out of his way to be a loving and attentive partner for the rest of the week. They didn't talk about Andrew for a couple of days, which at first had suited Cam. He wanted time to process what had gone on, without feeling pressured by his lover to move forward. On the one hand, he appreciated Ethan's sensitivity in this regard. On the other, it worried him a little, as Ethan wasn't the kind of guy to hold back what he was thinking. He could never keep secrets and he was a terrible liar. Cam knew he had to be dying to talk about the whole thing.

"About what?"

Cam took a breath, feeling like he was poised over a cold pool of water. He dove with, "Andrew's the real thing, isn't he?"

"A real Dom, you mean?"

"Yeah. He doesn't make false steps, like so many guys in the scene do. There's no posturing. I totally get your attraction to him. I felt it too. There's something about him. About his eyes, the way he looks at you..."

"Yeah. They're a cool color, too, right? Not exactly brown, it's like there's gold thrown in or something."

"Copper."

"Yeah. Copper. That's it." Ethan twisted toward Cam, who moved back to admire his handsome lover's features. The thick fringe of his eyelashes shadowed his cheeks and his hair looked almost silver in the moonlight.

Ethan said, "When he looks at you, it's like he sees past your face, you know what I mean? Like he's right inside your head, inside your secrets."

Cam nodded. "It's like he knows you. I mean *really* knows you, not your name, occupation, hobbies, quirks, but the stripped down essence of who you are."

"Yeah," Ethan whispered. They were silent for a while.

Cam snuggled back down against Ethan's chest. "That's what scares me," he finally ventured.

"Scares you?"

"Yeah. Because of us. We're both really attracted to this guy. Not just sexually, but as a Dom. That scene—it wasn't like the scenes at the clubs. We weren't playing. It was real. What does that mean for us as a couple? You know how compelling, how consuming, a relationship with a real Master can be. You kind of lose yourself, or you can, if you're not careful. If you and I get serious with this guy, how do we stop that from happening with each other? From losing what's special between us?"

There, he'd said it—laid it out in black and white. Ethan was quiet beside him for so long Cam thought he might have fallen back asleep. Finally Ethan said, "Are you saying you want that? A relationship with Andrew? Something more than just play dates at his dungeon?"

"I'm not sure what I'm saying. It's been six years since I was in a 24/7 D/s relationship. I thought Bryan was the real thing too. I mean, maybe he was, but the bottom line with us was, underneath the intense D/s thing, there wasn't a foundation of love. Maybe I was too young and stupid back then to even be in love, I don't know.

"Frankly, I decided back then that a 24/7 kind of thing just wasn't for me. That I was better off just doing the club thing and bringing the occasional Dom home for a night or two. Until I met you, I figured I was doomed never to be in a committed relationship, because I didn't want someone vanilla, but I didn't want to be owned, either.

"Then we got together, and you know what happened there—we both needed our kink. And I thought our solution was working pretty good, until this Maestro thing—"

"Cam, I'm sorry I didn't tell you right away—"

"No, please. I totally understand. If that had been me with him, shit, I would have probably done the same thing. He's a very compelling guy."

Ethan stroked Cam's hair. "Cam, let me ask you something."

"What?"

"Do you love me?"

"You know I do."

"Do you trust me?"

"With my life."

"Do you trust us?"

"What?"

"Do you trust us, as a couple? I'm feeling like maybe you don't. Like you think we're both going to dissolve into some kind of submissive zombies if we let ourselves get more involved with Andrew. Like we'll lose our identities as men and our connection as a couple."

"You haven't been there, Ethan. I mean in a committed 24/7 thing. It can be very intense."

"Okay. But we're not talking about that yet, are we?"

"No, I guess not. But if we agree to keep seeing this guy, it's the first step down that path. I want you to understand it's not something we should just step into lightly."

"Agreed. But I want you to trust us more. You and me. D/s is a choice, a consensual choice. We always have the right to stop whatever is happening. To step back, to step out, to end it. I'm not going to lie and say I don't want anything with Andrew. I do. I've been quiet this week to give you space, but you know it's been on my mind.

"I want to know what it's like, Cam. I want to be involved in something real. This is an amazing chance for us, you know? Kind of like we're getting our cake and eating it too. We stay together, but we get to have this experience with Andrew too. Not only that, we can share it. I'd like to think it would bring us closer, not push us apart."

Ethan pulled Cam up into his arms and kissed him until, one-by-one, every thought and every worry flew from his head.

~*~

Cam and Ethan were standing side-by-side in Andrew's dungeon, naked and at attention, eyes ahead, shoulders back, chins forward. Andrew stood in front of them. They'd agreed to keep their Friday night play date with Andrew, and see where things went from there. Andrew sat them down before taking them to the dungeon and they'd discussed limits. Cam still wasn't ready for anal intercourse with another man, but all three had agreed other anal play would be permitted, as well as oral sex.

Andrew reached for Ethan's throat, his long fingers gripping tightly. "Look at me," he commanded. Cam, too, turned his head, though he knew the command wasn't for him. Ethan's eyes were fixed on Andrew's. After a several long beats, they began to close. "Open your eyes. Focus. I'm going to count. You can do it." Andrew was squeezing hard, his action supremely dominant—a testament that, if he wanted, he could choke the life out of the submissive who had willingly handed over control.

"Three, two, one." Andrew let go, following up with a sharp slap to Ethan's cheek.

"What do you say?"

"Thank you, Sir." As Ethan spoke, he reached for his own shaft, which was sticking straight from his body.

Andrew slapped his hand away. "You know better than that. You don't touch without permission." Ethan dropped his hand back to his side, a sheepish look on his face.

Andrew moved to Cam. Though he knew what to expect from watching him with Ethan, he was unprepared for the strength of Andrew's grip around his own throat. It was so tight Cam couldn't even cough. Pressure began to build in his head and he began to get dizzy.

"Eyes open. Look at me," Andrew barked. Cam hadn't even realized he'd closed them. Another wave of dizziness passed through him and his legs began to buckle. "Three, two, one."

Andrew let go and, as he'd done with Ethan, slapped Cam's cheek hard, the sting spreading over his skin like fire. Because of who and what he was, this rough treatment caused an instant and raging erection above aching balls. He, too, wanted to stroke his cock but he did not. Instead he offered breathlessly, "Thank you, Sir."

Andrew went to the bureau and returned a moment later. He stood in front of Ethan. "You're familiar with these?" He held up a pair of clover clamps. Though Cam kept his face forward, he slid his eyes to the right, trying to see what Andrew was doing without being too obvious.

"Yes, Sir," Ethan answered. Andrew leaned down and flicked his tongue over Ethan's nipples, one at a time. He must have added teeth, because Ethan drew his breath sharply. When Andrew stepped back, Ethan's nipples were shiny and erect.

Pulling the nipple taut between thumb and forefinger, Andrew opened one of the clamps and let it close over it. Ethan winced and drew in a small, sharp breath. Andrew attached the second clamp to his other nipple and tugged at the chain between them.

"Oh," Ethan moaned.

"That's right. They tighten when I pull. Wonderful design. Leave it to the Japanese."

Andrew moved to Cam, who knew it was his turn. "These are different," Andrew said, holding up a second set of clamps. "They're designed for pierced nipples." He opened the clips at the end of the chain and attached them to the hoops at Cam's chest. "Not really fair, since the clamps on Ethan hurt all the time, while you'll only feel the pressure when they're pulled. But then, life isn't fair, is it?"

Assuming the question was rhetorical, Cam didn't answer. Andrew gave his chain a sharp jerk and Cam winced as his nipples were pulled taut. Perversely, his cock hardened in response to the erotic pain. Andrew apparently noticed this, because he slapped Cam's cock playfully and said, "Down, boy."

He dropped the chain and stepped back. "Face each other, arms behind your backs." Cam and Ethan obeyed. "Move closer." Andrew pulled something from his jeans pocket. Cam saw he held a metal clip, which he used to attach the two clamp chains together.

"Now step back," Andrew ordered.

Both Cam and Ethan took a pace back. Cam felt the tug on his nipples, though it didn't really hurt. Ethan, on the other hand, was clearly in pain, judging from the expression on his face. Like Cam, his cock was fully erect and pointing provocatively in Cam's direction.

"Again," Andrew said. They took another pace back and this time it hurt, the hoops straining against the sensitive nubbins.

"Ah," Ethan moaned, though his cock remained hard as ever.

"Maybe this will remind you not to come without permission," Andrew said, his voice low and seductive. He moved between them and hooked several lead fishing weights along the taut chains. Ethan's lips were pressed together, his eyes squeezed shut. Cam bit his lower lip to keep from crying out.

"And you," Andrew said, leaning close to Cam, "will learn to suck cock without letting him come. You'll learn to take him to the edge over and over, for hours if that's what I want. Think on that now, while your punishment continues."

"Yes, Sir," Cam breathed.

Andrew went to the whip wall and returned with a heavy flogger of shiny black leather. "Hands behind your heads. I'm going to whip you. Maintain your positions."

Andrew was wearing his black jeans again, but he was barefoot and shirtless. His torso was long and lean, the pecs sculpted and rising to broad shoulders. His skin had an olive tone and his chest was smooth, the nipples like round, caramel-colored coins against his muscular chest.

At first he stood beside them, reaching with his long arm to strike first Ethan's ass, then Cam's with the thuddy, slapping leather strands. Each stroke caused the chains between them to jerk, tugging at now numbing nipples.

After a while, Andrew moved behind Ethan, focusing solely on him. Cam watched, feeling each stroke as the chains jerked. He kept his hands behind his head, though what he most wanted to do was stroke his straining cock. Ethan's eyes were closed, his face a study in ecstasy. Andrew caught Cam's eye while he flogged Ethan. His expression was both fierce and filled with a longing that touched something in Cam.

After twenty or so strokes delivered to Ethan's back, ass and thighs, Andrew came around behind Cam, raining the heavy, stinging leather against his tingling flesh. He hit him hard, but Cam was ready and didn't move out of position. He loved a good flogging and could fly from it, if he was hit long enough.

Ethan opened his eyes, which slowly focused on Cam. They dropped to Cam's crotch and a small smile appeared on Ethan's lips. Cam was too distracted by the flogging to smile back.

All too soon for Cam, Andrew lowered his whipping arm and stepped to their side. He tucked the handle of the whip into the waist of his low-slung jeans. Cam and Ethan remained in position facing one another, fingers laced behind their necks, chests heaving, nipples throbbing, cocks bobbing.

Andrew removed the fishing weights. He reached for the clip and released it. Their respective chains fell back against their chests. Andrew lifted Cam's. "Open your mouth." Cam obeyed and Andrew pulled the chain taut, reawakening Cam's numbed nipples with the added tension. "Hold this between your teeth. Don't let it fall." Cam bit down on the chain that pulled hard on his nipple rings.

"You both did well, very well, for your first punishment. Of course, I'm not stupid enough to think it was really a punishment, since you both get off on the pain. A real punishment for sub boys like you is to be ignored and denied. Don't think I don't know it. But I think in this case the punishment suited the crime."

He moved toward Ethan and tugged at the chain hanging at his chest. "Ready?"

Ethan locked his diamond blue eyes on Andrew's and nodded, his expression intense. Cam felt a sympathetic tremor go through his own body when Andrew compressed and opened the clamps, allowing the blood flow to return, and along with it, the searing pain.

Ethan let out a long, shuddering breath, though to his credit, he remained in position. Cam knew he wanted nothing more than to massage his nipples, to rub away the sharp sting of reawakening nerves endings.

Cam was next. Andrew touched his cheek and said, "Open." Cam opened his mouth and the chain fell, slapping against his chest. "You got off easy," Andrew remarked, jerking suddenly against the chain, making Cam hiss at the unexpected arc of pain that shot through both nipples.

Andrew unclipped the clamps from the hoops. He walked back toward the bureau and dropped the clamps and weights into a drawer, stopping at the whipping wall to replace the flogger on its hook.

Returning to the guys, he asked, "How're we doing. Cam, you okay?"

Cam looked at Andrew. "Yes, Sir."

"Ethan? You good? Ready for more?"

Ethan nodded and grinned. "Yes, Sir."

It was a sign of a good Dom, to check periodically during a scene, not just by using his judgment, but actually hearing it from his sub's mouth. Cam silently approved but then he was distracted from his thought by what Andrew was doing. He was taking off his jeans, sliding them down his long, lean legs. He kicked them aside and Pulled his underwear off as well, revealing a long, thick cock already in a state of semi-erection.

He tossed them each a black eye mask, the kind used for sleeping. "Put those on and then kneel up, arms behind your backs, mouths open. You handled your punishment well and so you've earned the privilege of worshipping my cock. You're going to take turns at pleasing me. I'll decide who is the better cock sucker and you'll be rewarded, or punished, accordingly."

~*~

This is where they crossed the line. Cock sucking was not on the menu at the public clubs, falling under the category of exchange of bodily fluids. Lovers sucked each other's cocks. Was Andrew going to become their lover?

Ethan had been surprised but pleased when Cam had agreed not only to oral sex, but to anal play as well. Both Andrew and he had deferred to Cam during their discussion of limits, with a silent understanding that he was the one they needed to bring around.

Cam sure seemed to be enjoying himself so far. His cock looked like it could break a plank in half, it was so hard. Ethan wished they didn't have to wear the sleep masks—he wanted to watch Andrew's cock down Cam's throat. Cam could do amazing things with his throat muscles. Ethan figured it was a foregone conclusion he's lose this little competition, but he was prepared to give it his best shot.

His nipples still tingled from the clamps and his ass and back tingled pleasantly from the flogging. Mostly, though, his attention was drawn by his throbbing cock and aching balls. He was incredibly aroused and glad he wasn't being put to the test in the realm of orgasm control, as he knew he'd fail miserably and in short order.

He heard Andrew move close to him. "Find my cock," Andrew said. Ethan leaned forward, his tongue out, seeking the phallus. He made contact with the head and breathed in the intoxicating scent of an aroused man. Andrew smelled like soap and musk, with a hint of cloves. Greedily, Ethan sucked in the shaft.

Andrew's cock was longer than Cam's, though not quite as thick. Ethan did his best to relax his throat muscles, taking the full length of it. He was pleased when Andrew moaned, and redoubled his efforts, trying to imitate the massaging motion Cam used on him.

Andrew pulled back and Ethan instinctively leaned forward, trying to keep the shaft in his mouth. "Greedy boy." Andrew laughed. "Cam's turn."

Ethan settled back on his haunches, frustrated that he couldn't see. He could hear the slurping, gurgling sound of Cam's efforts, coupled with a series of groans of pleasure from Andrew's lips. Competitive by nature, Ethan itched to get that cock back and prove he could do better.

Within a minute or so, his wish was granted, Andrew's hard, wet cock being thrust back into his mouth. Andrew gripped his head, holding it still while he worked his rigid shaft in and out. He thrust hard and deep, making Ethan gag, though he couldn't pull back because of Andrew's grip in his hair.

Again the cock was withdrawn and Ethan could hear Cam at work, no sounds of gagging though. "Yeah," Andrew said, as if the word had been pulled from his mouth against his will. Suddenly the mask was pulled from Ethan's eyes. He blinked, adjusting to the sight of Andrew's big cock, his large hand pumping it.

"Keep your mouths open," he ordered. "Wide." Ethan obeyed, seeing Cam's mouth already in a round O. His mask had been removed as well. Cam was leaning forward, eager as a baby bird. Ethan leaned forward too, entranced by the sight of the tall, naked man jerking himself off just inches from their faces.

With a final moan, Andrew arched forward, shooting his copious seed first onto Cam's tongue and then Ethan's, warm, slightly bitter gobs of cum, which trailed over their cheeks as he moved from mouth to mouth, emptying his sac.

Andrew stood back, breathing hard. He surveyed the two subs still kneeling before him with glittering eyes. "Clean it up. Lick my cum from each other's faces." Ethan and Cam turned to each other. Cam's eyes were sparkling with an inner fire that Ethan had never seen before. He licked along the coarse auburn stubble of two day's growth at Cam's jaw, wiping away the smear of white, pearly semen left by Andrew. Cam licked him in turn, until they were both clean as kittens groomed by their mother.

Yet they continued to lick, their tongues now colliding and intertwining into a kiss neither had anticipated but neither could stop. All the pent-up desire created by the intense scene spilled over into that kiss. Along with the lust, Ethan felt gratitude, tremendous gratitude, both toward Andrew for providing him with such a thrilling and erotic experience, and Cam, for letting it happen.

Cam's arms came around him. He was sure Andrew would stop them, but he didn't, and so Ethan brought his arms around Cam, their kiss passionate, even desperate.

When at last they fell apart, Ethan turned to find Andrew.

The room was empty.

chapter 12

ANDREW LOOKED OUT the window at the city below him but he didn't see the buildings or the sky. He was focused inward, the image of Ethan and Cam locked in an embrace burned into his mind. Watching them kiss with such focused passion had rendered him invisible. He felt himself dissolving into thin air, shut out from their world so completely he might as well have been a ghost.

He'd pulled on a pair of jeans, not bothering with a shirt or underwear. He would wait for the guys to come out, thank them for the scene and send them on their way. Hopefully he wouldn't make an ass of himself in the process. Whatever else he had or didn't have, he still had his pride. He was damned if he'd let them see how much that kiss had hurt.

He hugged himself, wrapping his arms tight around his torso, as if that might somehow ease the pain. The ache of loneliness had completely usurped the intense pleasure of dominating two such responsive and sexy subs. Every aspect of the scene had unfolded with erotic perfection and heat.

Until that kiss.

In that one moment the stark reality of the situation slammed into him like a ton of bricks, shattering the glass wall he hadn't known was erected around his heart, and sending him reeling from the room. These men were lovers. Yes, they'd been into the scene, that was evident. But in the end, that's all it was for them—a scene. Nothing more.

Andrew bent forward, pressing his forehead against the cool window glass. He closed his eyes and permitted himself a long, low sigh.

He heard movement behind him and half hoped they'd just slip out the door—disappear and leave him to his quiet misery. Knowing this was unlikely, he girded himself for a different kind of scene—putting on a false front and pretending everything was fine.

Yeah, thanks for the scene, see you around...

He felt something on the back of his leg and a moment later on the other leg as well. Twisting back, he saw Ethan's white-blond head and Cam's auburn curls. Both naked, they were kneeling at his feet, their bowed heads touching the backs of his calves.

"Oh," he said in surprise.

They looked up at him at the same time, and the light he saw shining in their eyes nearly took his breath away. As if they'd planned it, each man lifted his arms and wrapped them around Andrew's knees, resting their cheeks against his thighs.

Overcome by the sweet, silent eloquence of the gesture, Andrew reached down and pulled them both up into his arms.

~*~

It had been confusing to break from their impromptu kiss and find Andrew gone. Ethan had speculated he was angry because they'd strayed from his control by kissing one another without permission.

But Cam offered the more likely reason—he was feeling left out. The kiss had highlighted the fact they were lovers, shattering the illusion he was part of that love. Maybe they couldn't offer him love, but they could offer submissive devotion. Both still caught up in the rapture of the scene, endorphins zinging through their bloodstreams, they'd gone in search of their Dom.

In those few seconds before he'd reached down to them, Cam had recognized just how much it mattered to him—not just for Ethan's sake, but for his own.

They'd stood in a shared embrace for several long moments. Andrew was the one to pull away. Though both Ethan and Cam had wanted to stay longer, Andrew had them dress and sent them on their way within a few minutes, claiming he had to be somewhere. They'd left, not wanting to force the issue.

It had been three days and they hadn't heard a word from Andrew. Cam began to think he wasn't going to call. He tried to tell himself it was for the best. Andrew was an exciting addition to their lives, but by the same token he was a dangerous one.

Outwardly Ethan acted as if it wasn't that big a deal, but Cam knew he was upset too. There was a pall over their weekend until Monday night when Ethan's cell phone rang.

The look of pure joy on Ethan's face was priceless.

"He says he's sorry he wasn't in touch sooner." Ethan reported, once they'd hung up. "He's inviting us to a private play party being hosted by Samurai! Get this, it's at Samurai's penthouse suite on Central Park West! It's on Thursday and—" Ethan cut himself off, hitting his forehead. "Crap! I can't go. I have that conference in Boston and then a dinner afterwards with some important new clients from Japan. Roger's already booked us hotel rooms for Thursday night because he says last time he took these guys out to dinner, they stayed out drinking until one in the morning. He worked his ass off to get their account and he wants to make sure they have a good time."

"Can't you get out of it?" Cam said with more urgency than he'd intended. His cock was stirring to attention, his mind leaping back to their Friday night. They could pretend to each other all they wanted that it was for the best that Andrew fade away, but Cam knew that was a lie. Not to mention, the party sounded fun.

Ethan shook his head. "I would love to, believe me, but this one's in my area of expertise and Roger was pretty adamant about me going. As easygoing as Roger is about most things, I don't dare risk making something up to get out of this one."

Cam tried to keep his tone light, denying even to himself the rush of intense disappointment he felt. "Ah well. We'll have other chances."

"Hey, just because I can't make it, doesn't mean you can't. We could see if that was all right with Andrew."

Cam did a mental double take. It honestly hadn't occurred to him that was even an option. Though he was becoming involved, both physically and emotionally, with Andrew, he thought of the Dom as "belonging" to Ethan. Ethan had had him first and Ethan was, after all, the one Andrew really wanted. Cam didn't fool himself otherwise, even though the one-on-one play with Andrew had been intense and had deeply affected him.

"I can?" he said stupidly.

"Why not? No reason you should sit home alone just because I can't make it. It's not like I don't trust you. This is a way back for us with him. Andrew's reaching out. I say, go for it. Unless, of course, you don't want to or you have other plans."

"No way," Cam said a little too quickly. Backing off, he added, "I mean, it's a Thursday, so it's not like I have any club dates planned or whatever. Not that I'm even interested at this point."

"Yeah, I know what you mean. After the scenes with Andrew, it's kind of hard to think of going back to amateur hour at the clubs."

The thought of seeing Andrew again had caused Cam's cock to spring awake. It was Monday and they hadn't made love since Friday night when they'd left Andrew's. It wasn't even really making love that night—they were both too confused and upset by Andrew's abrupt dismissal. It was more of a release from the pent-up lust Andrew had stirred in them both. It was mutual masturbation.

Ethan looked at the bulge in Cam's pants and a seductive smile lifted the corners of his mouth. Cam moved toward and dropped his hand to Ethan's crotch, pressing the palm flat against the front of his pants.

Ethan moaned appreciatively and thrust his pelvis forward, forcing his rapidly hardening cock against Cam's hand. At the same time, he pulled Cam close and kissed him. They began to pull at each other's clothing, stripping as they stumbled toward the bedroom, hungry for each other's touch, fueled by Andrew's call and their shared memories.

Cam realized his mouth was open and he snapped it shut. The living room of Samurai's penthouse suite was bigger than their entire Brooklyn apartment. The walls of the room were curved, two thirds of them one huge convex window, offering a breathtaking view of the brilliantly lit Manhattan skyline.

They'd given their names and destination to the guard inside the lobby of the elegant apartment building. After asking for their ID, he consulted a mini-laptop that rested on the marbled countertop. "You may go up. You're expected." The guard's face was impassive as his eyes flickered over tall, handsome Andrew in his tight black leather pants and red silk pirate shirt opened at the throat, and Cam beside him wearing jeans and an olive-drab cotton sports jacket with nothing beneath except a slim black collar of leather at his throat and the gold glinting at his nipples. With Samurai as a prime tenant, this guy had probably seen everything.

Borrowing Ethan's car, Cam had made the trip from Brooklyn to Manhattan, meeting Andrew first at his apartment. Andrew had explained Samurai's party rule—all subs were required to wear a collar to enter. When Cam had arrived at Andrew's apartment, Andrew had presented him with the collar he now wore.

Despite knowing this collar was just part of his costume for the evening, Cam couldn't help the submissive tremor that went through his body when Andrew stood just behind him, buckling it into place. He hadn't worn a collar since his days with Bryan. Just the feeling of the stiff leather tightening around his throat made him hard.

Andrew must have sensed his reaction, because afterwards he put his arms around Cam for a moment and leaned down, speaking softly in Cam's ear. "Maybe one day you'll wear my collar permanently, both you and Ethan." He moved his hands beneath Cam's jacket, stroking his chest.

"The collar signifies that you belong to me for the evening. Does that suit you?"

"Yes, Sir," Cam whispered.

"And do you want to submit to me in front of witnesses? To prove your submission in a public scene, if it pleases me?"

Cam's heart was thumping pleasantly against his chest, his cock already rising in anticipation. "Yes, Sir," he repeated.

"Good boy," Andrew had said, and then, stepping back, "We should go. Samurai's got a Japanese thing about punctuality. He'll take it as an insult if we're late."

After a ride up in an elevator paneled in rich wood with a real crystal chandelier hanging from its ceiling, they walked down a thickly-carpeted hallway toward the only door on the floor. When Andrew rang the bell, they were greeted by a dark-skinned, handsome man with long black hair plaited in braids and pulled back in a thick ponytail. He was naked, save for thin strips of black leather, criss-crossed tightly over his prominent cock and balls. Cam noticed his arms, chest and thighs were covered in myriad small cuts in various stages of healing.

"Welcome," the man said. "I'm Gordon, Samurai's slave."

There were maybe twenty other men in the room, each one better looking than the last. A strikingly handsome Asian man of medium height extracted himself from a small group of guys and moved toward them with a smile. He was wearing a burgundy jacket over a cream-colored silk vest and matching cream silk slacks. His feet were bare.

"Andrew, I'm so glad you could come." He had no accent to speak of, but spoke in the clipped, precise way of someone for whom English was not their native tongue. Cam surmised this must be their host, the famous Samurai.

"Thank you for inviting me." Andrew bowed, Asian-style, toward the man, who bowed back with a small but warm smile. "This is Cam." Andrew put his arm lightly around Cam's shoulders.

Samurai turned toward Cam, openly raking his body with a bold stare. He glanced at the leather collar at Cam's throat and fixed Cam with narrow black eyes. Cam could feel power radiating from the man. He found he had a sudden odd impulse to kneel in front of him and plant a kiss on one of those bare feet. Instead he leaned against Andrew.

Samurai arched one eyebrow. "Very, *very* nice to meet you, Cam," he said, flashing a wolfish smile.

"And you, Sir," Cam said. "I've heard great things about the Red Dragon over the years."

Samurai nodded, directing himself toward Andrew. "Perhaps you can bring this boy with you one evening. We could put him through his paces on the rack, hmm?"

Andrew looked at Cam. "Would you like that?"

"Yes, Sir," Cam replied, his curiosity piquing at the thought of gaining entrance to the trendy, exclusive club.

A blond muscular man appeared beside them, wearing only a white loincloth, a thick link of chain secured around his neck with a padlock. He was holding a silver tray with two crystal champagne flutes balanced on it.

"Champagne, Sir?" The man gave a deferential bow toward Andrew, ignoring Cam completely. Letting go of Cam's shoulders, Andrew took the glasses and offered one to Cam. He sipped it, trying not to stare at the cut marks on Gordon's body.

New guests were arriving and Samurai excused himself to greet them. Cam noticed there were a several other men wearing the uniform of loincloth and chain, moving among the guests, exchanging full glasses for empty.

Cam turned to Andrew. "So you can get in any time at Red Dragon? How'd you swing that?"

Andrew smiled. "A little known secret—I went to school with Samurai at the Stevens Institute back in New Jersey. That's where we met. He went by the name Hiro back then, his given name. He actually has a degree in chemical engineering but as far as I know, he's never worked a day in his life. He's independently wealthy, but his family believes strongly in education.

"We dated for a few months in college and back then he was a sub, believe it or not. He's become quite the sadist since he made the switch." Andrew gave a dry laugh. "It's been my experience that the most brutal Doms were once subs. I'm not sure why that is."

"What makes him so brutal?"

"He's into edge play, big time. Knife play. You probably noticed the cuts on Gordon's body. He'll do a demonstration later, for those who are interested. It's not really my thing, but if you want—"

"No thanks," Cam averred, shivering. "Not my thing either." Cam had once witnessed that sort of edge play at a private party at a friend of Bryan's years before. Using a razor knife, a Dom had drawn red lines along his sub's chest, arms and legs. At first Cam had though he was using a marker of some kind. Then, as bright droplets of red blood had beaded along the lines, he'd understood with dawning horror what he was witnessing.

It was all consensual and when the Dom was done, he'd jerked the sub off in about thirty seconds flat and then had the sub lick the cum from the Dom's fingers. Bryan had teasingly suggested they try that at home, but Cam had refused and to his relief, Bryan hadn't pressed the matter.

"There'll be plenty of other action, don't worry," Andrew said. "Maybe we'll provide a little entertainment of our own." He put his arm around Cam again, letting his hand drop to Cam's chest. Pushing back the jacket, he found and lightly tugged at one of Cam's nipple rings. Cam's cock responded at once to the tug at his nerve endings and he licked his lips in silent anticipation of the night ahead.

For a while they just mingled in the spacious room. Andrew knew a number of the people there and Cam saw several guys he recognized from the underground clubs. After a while Cam noticed there were fewer people in the room, though more had been arriving over the half-hour or so they'd been there.

"They've gone off to do private scenes," Andrew explained. "Samurai has a fully equipped dungeon and several bedrooms he makes available for play. This room is pretty much just for hanging out. You'd almost think it was a regular party if you stayed in here the whole time."

Almost, but not quite. There were a number of men who were naked or nearly so, trussed in cock cages or bound in chain and rope. Though there were no overt scenes going on, there was posturing between Doms showing off their sub boys, some of whom were made to kneel and beg for their food, their hands lifted like dog paws at their chests, mouths open for the delicious morsels of food.

The food was incredible—everything from Beluga caviar to exquisitely prepared sushi to the best crème brulée Cam had ever tasted. The champagne was flowing freely, a new glass appearing on a silver tray each time his was empty.

"That's Jermaine," Andrew said, nodding toward a powerfully built man with a shaved head. He wore a black biker jacket over black pants and boots. A small duffel bag was slung over his shoulder. Just behind him were two men, both blond and slender, their hands chained behind their backs. They were being led from the living room by leashes clipped to their thick leather collars. Other than the collar and chains they were naked and smooth as babes.

"He owns those two guys," Andrew said. "They aren't his lovers, just his slaves. He's big into orgasm denial and control. Which can have its place, of course, but he takes it to extremes. Still, he usually has some interesting new toy or other he likes to demonstrate. I'm curious what he's got in that bag tonight. Want to check it out?"

"Sure." Cam nodded, thinking back to his own "slave days" and how the lack of love had drained the richness, at least for him, of a D/s relationship. Still, watching a hot scene would be fun.

They followed Jermaine and his slave boys down a long hallway toward a room about halfway down. It was a bedroom, but instead of a bed, there were two restraint tables with leather cuffs placed at intervals along them. Across from the tables were a sofa and a love seat.

Jermaine entered first, followed by the two men. Placing the duffel on one of the restraint tables, Jermaine stopped in the center of the room and pointed at his feet. Both men dropped at once to the ground. Crouching down with heads to the ground, they fell to licking Jermaine's scuffed boots like the leather was ice cream.

Four other guys, two Doms and two subs, along with Andrew and Cam, had trailed after Jermaine, no doubt also eager to watch the show. The Doms sat on the sofa, their subs at their feet. No one spoke. Andrew and Cam sat on the loveseat and Andrew dropped his hand to Cam's thigh.

With blond heads bobbing at his feet, Jermaine turned to the audience and smiled briefly, though his eyes looked hard. There was something cold about him, something forbidding that made Cam glad he wasn't one of those guys on his knees.

One of the guys began to tongue his way up the man's leg. The other slave quickly followed suit, licking in broad, flat strokes against the rough fabric. When they were both at thigh level, Jermaine opened his fly, letting a large, uncircumcised cock spring free.

The boys began to fight for it, licking and sucking in a frenzy, butting each other with their heads to get the better angle. Throughout the display, Jermaine remained impassive, save for a slight press of his lips and narrowing of his eyes.

After a few minutes, he placed a large hand on each sub's head and pushed. They fell back, both losing their balance, unable to break their falls because of their chained wrists. Jermaine laughed and Cam's reservation bloomed into dislike. He understood and indeed craved sensual control and erotic suffering, but he didn't like that sort of humiliation.

Apparently the slave boys did, however, because both of them had rock-hard cocks. "Get in position," Jermaine barked as he tucked himself into his jeans. Both guys scrambled up as best they could with shackled wrists, managing to hoist themselves onto their knees on the tables.

Cam saw their skin was marked with welts, some faded, some fresh. Their shaven balls hung swinging between their legs, their bare, splayed asses facing the audience. Jermaine unzipped his bag and withdrew two identical implements. They were made from polished stainless steel, with fat conical heads about the size of a small egg at the end of a T handlebar.

Jermaine took a tube of lubricant and squirted a dollop on each metal head. "He's going to massage their prostates. His orgasm denial thing." Andrew whispered, the grip on Cam's thigh tightening. "Anyone ever do that to you?"

"Yeah," Cam answered, though he knew it as milking. Bryan did it as punishment. By applying a constant, massaging pressure against the prostate from inside the ass, it was possible to force the seminal fluid out of the cock, without the pleasure of an orgasm.

Cam fidgeted beside Andrew as Jermaine inserted the milking tools, none too gently, into his slaves' asses. He pushed until nearly the entire silver handles were embedded, before slowly pulling them back. He pushed them in again, leaving them sticking lewdly from the men's behinds while he moved in front of them. Though Cam couldn't see precisely what he was doing, he guessed Jermaine was stroking their cocks, getting them sufficiently hard so the onlookers could see the show.

When he stepped away, it was possible to see their erect cocks from behind, the heads hanging below the swaying balls. As he milked them, a thin line of ejaculate began to trail from each man's cock, dripping onto the metal restraint tables.

Jermaine probed their asses for several minutes, during which nobody moved or spoke. The room was silent save for the occasional grunt or moan from one of the slaves. When Jermaine was satisfied, he withdrew the anal probes and ordered, "Lick it up."

Both guys contorted, shifting and nearly falling from the tables in their effort to obey. Cam was thrust back in time. He was Bryan's slave boy, forced to scuttle between Bryan's friends and lick their ejaculate from the floor as they jerked off in a circle around him. Cam realized he was clenching his jaw. He shook his head, willing away the memory.

Looking from the slaves to their Master, the expression he saw there was the same one that had glinted from Bryan's eyes. It was triumphant. An expression of power, of conquest, without a trace of love. Cam shivered and hugged himself, feeling suddenly twenty-two again and very lonely.

He wished desperately that Ethan was there. Ethan would understand.

Andrew was no longer watching the action. He was watching Cam. He touched the back of Cam's hand with two fingers, his expression filled with a tenderness that made Cam's heart clutch. *I'm sorry,* it seemed to say.

Cam shifted and Andrew's hand fell away. "Let's get out of here," he said in an undertone. He stood as Jermaine was taking two single tail lashes from his bag.

Cam nodded gratefully. They left the room, closing the door behind them with a snick. Cam turned to walk down the hall back toward the living room but Andrew stopped him, pressing him gently against the wall.

"You were upset in there." It wasn't a question.

"Yeah. Not my thing, I guess."

Andrew seemed to be waiting for him to say more, but when Cam didn't elaborate, he said, "I know what you mean. You see a lot of that at the clubs. It isn't about an erotic exchange. It's just a claiming. Exerting power because you can. There's no passion in it. No..."

"Love," Cam supplied.

"Yes," Andrew said softly.

He leaned down, his face so close Cam could feel his warm breath on his cheek. Despite himself, his lips parted, tingling for the kiss he was suddenly longing for. Andrew dipped his head closer and Cam closed his eyes, lifting his face.

No kiss came. Instead he felt the faint swish of air as Andrew moved abruptly back, dropping his arms to his sides. Cam opened his eyes, embarrassed and confused.

"Come on," Andrew said, his voice suddenly gruff. "You said you wanted a scene. Let's show them our brand of submission."

chapter 13

THE DOOR WAS ajar and, after giving a little knock, Andrew pushed it open and entered. It was a kind of den, with several large sofas and chairs set about the room, arranged in a semi-circle facing each other.

There were three other couples already in the room. Two of the subs were on their knees with their Doms' cocks in their mouths, though they weren't sucking them off, but rather were still as statues, their arms clasped behind their backs.

The two men who were seated were carrying on a conversation as if they didn't have their cocks shoved down their sub boys' throats. The third couple was sitting on a sofa, the sub's arms bound behind his back, a fat purple ball gag wedged between his lips. He wore a lace-up leather cock sheath with studs, his shaven balls prominently exposed beneath. His Dom was idly flicking his bare chest with a small, wicked-looking quirt.

Andrew and Cam entered the room. "Hello, Jacob." Andrew nodded toward the man with the bound and gagged sub beside him.

"Andrew Townsend. Long time. Great party, huh? Who's the redhead?"

"This is Cam. For tonight at least, Cam belongs to me." He turned to Cam, losing himself for a moment in those vivid green eyes. He had come *that* close to kissing Cam. Though he'd been extremely physically attracted to Cam from the moment he'd laid eyes on him, he hadn't experienced the intense emotional connection he had with Ethan. But something had changed between them just now—something vital.

It had happened while he was watching Cam's reaction to the display of cold, empty power Jermaine offered. He had sensed the tension in Cam's body, which increased as the scene unfolded. Observing him from the corner of his eye, he'd seen the pain flit over Cam's face. Somehow this had reached Andrew on a much deeper level than if Cam had shown excitement, arousal or even fear.

For the first time since he'd reconnected with Ethan, Andrew considered the possibility of Cam on his own terms. Cam without Ethan. Watching Cam's sensitive response to the scene, Andrew had begun the first tumble down the hill of love.

Cam looked down, breaking the stare between them and jerking Andrew back to the present. He moved toward the empty sofa and sat down. Cam wanted a public scene, and Cam would have it—not like Jermaine's clinical abuse, but a hot, sexy, hands-on spanking.

Pushing away the new emotions he felt toward Cam, Andrew focused on the physical. No matter how you sliced it, Cam was a very hot package. Andrew decided to show off the younger man's sculpted abs, pierced nipples and hot little ass. After all, he was his, at least for that one night.

"Take off your jacket," he said. He waited while Cam complied, folding his jacket neatly over an arm of the sofa. All eyes were on the handsome sub and Andrew felt a surge of pride, as if he really belonged to him, and wasn't just on loan for this scene and others like it.

"Kneel in front of me, arms behind your back."

Cam slid gracefully to his knees, his eyes downcast. Andrew sat forward and reached for Cam's throat, wrapping his fingers around it, adding just enough pressure to get his attention.

"Look at me," he commanded.

Cam looked up, his lips parting, an expression of rapture settling over his face, even as it reddened. Andrew knew he couldn't breathe. He counted in his head, squeezing hard now, sensitive to the slightest resistance or distress from the sub. There was none. On the contrary, Andrew recognized by Cam's adoring gaze that he would stay that way until he passed out. He glanced down at Cam's crotch, the bulge leaving no question as to his desire.

Andrew released his throat. Cam took a deep breath, his eyes fixed on Andrew's. Before he could stop himself, Andrew grabbed Cam by the back of head and pulled him close.

He wanted to kiss him. No, more than that, he wanted to push him down then and there, oblivious to the gawking onlookers. He wanted to rip those jeans from his body and fuck him. His balls ached and the hunger he felt had nothing to do with food. What was happening to him? There was way too much emotion surging through him. He needed to regain control. He needed to focus on the scene.

He let Cam go and drew in a breath. They had an audience who expected a show. Patting his thigh, he said. "Drop your pants and lie over my lap. I'm in the mood to give you a good, old-fashioned spanking."

Everyone watched as Cam kicked off his shoes, unbuttoned his fly and slid out of his jeans. He wore a black thong that hugged the very obvious erection and full balls beneath. The only sound in the room was the slurping gasps of the two subs on their knees, who were now sucking their Doms' cocks in earnest.

Gracefully, Cam draped himself over Andrew's lap. Andrew could feel the steel of Cam's erection, which matched his own. Cam held his body stiffly, his muscles tensed. Andrew leaned over, murmuring, "Relax."

Closing his eyes, Andrew forgot there were other people in the room as he stroked Cam's firm, supple flesh. Running his hands over Cam's ass and lower back, he willed the muscles in Cam's body to relax. They began to ease beneath his touch, though Cam's cock remained hard against his leg.

Andrew's palms fairly itched with anticipation. He began lightly at first, alternately rubbing and lightly smacking Cam's ass cheeks. He waited until all the tension had eased from Cam's body before the first real blow. He brought his open hand down hard on one cheek, the sound cracking the air.

Cam jerked and took a second blow, harder than the first, on his other cheek. "Thank you, Sir," he gasped.

Andrew smiled. "You're welcome."

He settled into the rhythm, thrilling to Cam's reddening flesh, his breathy, sensual sighs and the iron of his cock, mashing against Andrew's leg with each blow. Cam began to pant when Andrew changed the shape of his hand, cupping the palm to increase the sting. He used his hand like a wooden paddle, smacking relentlessly against increasingly tender flesh.

"That's it," Andrew crooned. "Breathe through the pain. Stop wiggling. Take what I give you. You can do it. I know you can. Let yourself go where you need to go." Andrew well knew that a firm spanking could be harder to take than a whipping. A man's large hand covered more surface area than a whip or even a flogger.

"Oh, oh, oh," Cam began to chant, an edge of panic tingeing his cry. Andrew eased off a moment, running his hands lightly over Cam's ass. He wanted to lick the heated skin, but of course he did no such thing. Instead he asked softly, "Are you okay, Cam? Is this too much?"

"No, Sir," Cam managed between ragged breaths.

"Shall I continue?"

"Yes. Yes, *please*, Sir."

The plea was heartfelt and Andrew understood. It was the delicious irony of a masochist's lot. It wasn't too much, even when it was. He knew if Cam could just work his way through the pain, he would come out on the other side into a state of ecstasy.

There wasn't a sound in the room. Even the sub boys who had been sucking their Doms' cocks were still.

Andrew could feel Cam's shaft poking hard against his thigh. "Lift your hips a second." Cam obeyed and Andrew hooked his fingers beneath the waist of Cam's thong and pulled, dragging it down to his thighs. His bare cock and balls now rubbed directly against Andrew's legs each time his hard hand landed on Cam's ass or thighs.

Andrew was smacking him hard in a steady, slow rhythm, each blow pulling a grunt from Cam's lips. All at once, Cam's breathing slowed dramatically. His muscles relaxed, the deadweight of his body melting against Andrew. Andrew knew he had entered that sacred zone where pleasure and pain meld together, floating toward the sublime.

He let Cam drift awhile in his private submissive heaven, keeping him there with well-placed smacks. Cam's cock was hard against his leg. He wanted to roll Cam over and suck it until Cam cried for mercy. If they'd been lovers, instead of players in a public scene, he would have done just that.

Instead, Andrew parted his legs and shifted, catching Cam's cock between them. He squeezed and the pressure, coupled with the spankings, made Cam groan aloud. Andrew began to smack him in a rapid, sharp tattoo, each stroke jerking his cock between Andrew's legs.

All at once, Cam began to shudder in a series of uncontrollable tremors before finally stilling. Andrew knew what had happened. His very naughty slave boy had come without permission.

"Oh dear," he said with mock dismay.

"Shit," Cam whispered. When he twisted back to look at Andrew, Andrew saw that he was blushing. He wanted to gather the sexy sub into his arms and kiss him. "I'm sorry, Sir," Cam murmured apologetically. "It just happened. I didn't mean to."

"I know," Andrew said, unable to maintain his stern visage. He gave Cam a gentle push and Cam rolled to the ground, where he knelt, his head bowed, his underwear still tangled at his thighs.

The other men in the room began to realize what had happened. One of the Doms said in a loud, mocking voice, "Someone is due for a serious punishment." The other men laughed. Cam kept his head bowed, the very picture of erotic humiliation.

Andrew used the tail of his shirt to wipe away the blobs of semen Cam had left on his pants. Instead of being angry at Cam for coming without permission, he was turned on by it. If they'd been alone and Cam had been his lover, he would have pulled out his cock and let the sub boy worship it.

Instead he stood, patting Cam's head. "Get up and put on your things. It's time to go." Cam stood unsteadily, which reminded Andrew he'd had quite a bit of champagne. Andrew, who never drank much at this kind of party, had had only one glass, switching afterward to soda.

Cam pulled up his thong and reached for his jeans, his face still flushed. The other guys in the room continued to laugh derisively and offer unsolicited advice about how Cam should be punished. Andrew ignored them, helping Cam into his sports jacket. Cam still didn't seem quite steady on his feet. Putting a supportive arm around him, Andrew led Cam from the room.

Once they were in the hall, Cam began, "I'm really sorry, Sir," but Andrew cut him off with two fingers pressed lightly against his lips.

"It's okay. I didn't tell you that you couldn't come. I think you did great under the circumstances. You took a very intense spanking in front of others. I was proud to be your Dom in there. Are you ready to leave?"

At that moment Andrew wanted nothing more than to get away from the crowd, the noise, the casual indifference of this group of players. What used to seem so glamorous and cutting edge now felt tawdry and overdone.

He was glad when Cam nodded. "Yes, Sir. I'm ready."

The question was, ready for what?

~*~

Cam waited while Andrew unlocked the front door. He had mixed feelings about coming up to Andrew's apartment. Andrew had insisted on driving from the party, and Cam had to admit he was still a little tipsy from the champagne. Ethan liked to tease him that he was a "cheap date", as it didn't take much to get him drunk.

It wasn't that Cam didn't want to spend more time with Andrew. No. It was the opposite. He was afraid if he went inside, he might do something they would regret. He might betray his promise to Ethan—the promise that had overarched their relationship and allowed them to scene with Doms and still trust each other.

Yet he couldn't deny the powerful draw of the handsome Dom beside him, made all the more powerful by the sensitivity he'd shown at the party. Something was different now, there was no question about that.

Cam tried to put his finger on when the change between them had occurred. It was subtle but powerful—a shift in the way they reacted to each other. It had happened, Cam decided, when Jermaine began his scene.

Cam had hated watching the twin slave boys, but he'd sat through it for Andrew's sake, aware he was probably only reacting to bad memories with Bryan. But when he'd looked at Andrew, expecting to see him riveted to the action, instead he'd found Andrew looking at *him* with an expression of such tenderness and compassion it nearly took Cam's breath away.

It was as if he understood, without the need for Cam to say a word. Ethan and Cam sometimes despaired of there being any real Doms out there—Doms who understood and appreciated the romance of D/s, along with the power. He'd felt both from Andrew tonight.

The spanking, while on its surface was just another in a series of scenes at a party, had felt very different to Cam. Tonight, for the first time in a long time, Cam had ascended to that physiological and emotional level of pure, utter peace. Not only that, he'd done it in public, with a man he'd never even kissed. It occurred to him the champagne might have played a part, but he didn't really think so.

He'd been floating in the heavenly place when Andrew had recaptured his attention by catching Cam's cock between his legs, creating an exquisite friction. Cam, already so aroused from the spanking and the continued rub of Andrew's strong thighs against his cock and balls, lost control. He had been powerless to resist the climax that shuddered through him, his body taken over, owned by that hard palm and those strong legs.

He'd expected Andrew's disappointment at his lack of control, or at least his annoyance at the cum stains on his fancy leather pants. But Andrew had only smiled, his lips moving in a soft upward curve, though his eyes blazed with a coppery fire.

"Come in and sit down. I'll get us some coffee," Andrew said, ushering Cam into his place. Cam sat on the sofa he'd sat on with Ethan. He thought back to their first time here, and how nervous and excited he'd been at sharing a scene with Ethan for the first time.

He thought about calling Ethan just to see how he was doing. He pulled his cell phone from his jacket and realized it was dead. "Don't forget to charge your phone," Ethan had reminded him just before he'd left that morning. He'd honestly meant to that morning, but something had distracted him and it had slipped his mind.

He thought about asking to use Andrew's phone, but decided against it. Though his being in Andrew's apartment alone and without Ethan was perfectly innocent, why thrust it in Ethan's face? Why remind him of his own enforced absence?

Andrew came in with a tray containing two mugs of coffee, a spoon, a pint of cream and a few packets of sugar. He set it on the low coffee table in front of them and sat down beside Cam. Cam resisted the impulse to press his thigh against Andrew's.

Instead he reached for a mug. Tearing open two packets of sugar, he emptied them into the mug and stirred in some cream. Andrew, he noted, drank his black.

They made small talk for a while about the party and people they knew there. Andrew set down his mug and turned to face Cam. "You were flying tonight, weren't you? It was really something, feeling the change come over you like that."

"You could tell?" Cam put his mug down and shifted to face Andrew.

"Sure. It's not something you could miss. It's like someone gives you a shot of morphine or something—everything just eases off, slows down. It's really pretty amazing to watch. And when you're the Dom who made it happen, it's a high like no other."

"Tell me more," Cam said, intrigued. He'd often dissected the experience of flying with other subs, including Ethan, but he'd never really thought about it from a Dom's point of view.

"Well," Andrew said, leaning back against the sofa and looking up at the ceiling as he gathered his thoughts. "I think of it like taming a wild horse. The whipping or whatever you're doing to the sub stimulates them to the point they're out of control—bucking, panting, maybe crying out—all because of what you're doing to them. It's like they have to move beyond a certain point of pain before they can rise up into this other place."

"Yes," Cam interjected. "That's how I think of it. You have to descend into the pain before you can rise into the pleasure."

Andrew nodded. "It's amazing to watch. As a Dom, you have to be careful not to take your sub too far. Because when they get to that point, they lose perspective. They even lose the ability to gauge what they're feeling. I mean physically, they're in this space, where they literally don't experience the pain as pain anymore, am I right?"

"Exactly right. It's almost like you get numb. I mean, I'm sure that's part of it—the physiological part—your skin becomes numb as the endorphins rush through you, I guess. But it's more than that. It's almost like you fall away from your body. That's why I call it flying. It feels like I've left my body, like I'm hovering over it, flying in a clear, blue, peaceful place. I never want it to stop."

"Right. That's why it's so important for a Dom to really listen to his sub's reactions and to his body. We have to decide when you're had enough. You greedy subs would just go on forever."

Cam laughed, knowing this was true. Andrew laughed too. They sipped their coffee in a companionable silence for a while, each lost in his own thoughts. Cam was thinking of Ethan. He wished his lover was there to share this time with Andrew. It was nice, just getting to know him without the overlay of a scene to deal with.

What would it be like to make love to Andrew, not as Dom and sub, but just as men? The thought startled Cam and then made him feel guilty. What was he thinking?

"I'd like you to stay tonight, Cam," Andrew said softly. "Not for sex," he added hurriedly, as if anticipating Cam's protest. "We'll wait for Ethan for that. But it's late, you've had a lot to drink and there's no real reason to drive home tonight is there? Ethan's not due back till the afternoon, right?"

"I don't know," Cam said hesitantly. It wasn't that he didn't want to stay the night. It was that he wanted to way too much, and he knew it. What the hell was going on? He loved *Ethan*. This was a chance to know Andrew better, sure, but not at a cost to his relationship with Ethan.

But would the feelings go away, just because he ignored them? And anyway, they were grown men. They could spend a night without losing control. Couldn't they?

Andrew stood. "Let's lie down. Just rest a while."

"Oh, I've heard that before." Cam laughed.

"Hey," Andrew said, lifting his arms up with open hands to indicate his innocence. "This is not an attempt to seduce you, I promise. We'll even lie on top of the sheets, fully clothed. Deal?"

Cam shrugged. What the hell? Andrew was right. Why risk driving with alcohol still in his system? It had been a long day and he was exhausted. Lying down for a while was a good idea. Keeping their clothes on was an even better idea, as he knew if he got naked with Andrew, Andrew would be the one having to fight him off, not vice versa.

Andrew changed out of his leather and silk, putting on a T-shirt and a pair of soft cotton shorts. They lay down on the bed and Andrew reached for Cam, pulling his head down onto his chest, unaware this was how Ethan and Cam often slept, with Cam in just this position.

It was strange to lie in the dark with a man who wasn't Ethan, a different heartbeat thrumming against his cheek. At the same time, it felt good to be in Andrew's arms. Andrew stroked his hair in a soothing gesture. Cam's eyes drooped, his body relaxing.

"I have a confession." Andrew's voice pulled Cam from the brink of sleep.

"What?"

"Before I met you. No, even after I met you, I had this vague plan to steal Ethan away from you." Cam was fully awake now, though he said nothing. "I would have seduced him that first day when we kissed, if he hadn't refused. I think I'd carried this fantasy of him in my head for so many years that in some twisted way I felt like he was already mine. You were the interloper, not me. I just had to win him back. To make him see we were supposed to be together."

Still Cam said nothing, though his gut twisted. Andrew continued. "Even when we had the first dungeon scene, though I found you incredibly sexy as a sub, I still harbored thoughts of stealing him away.

"The second time was different. I actually realized I wanted you both. Not just as subs, but as lovers. But I also recognized how deeply in love with each other you were. I knew then I could never have Ethan, not while his heart belonged to you."

Cam knew Ethan craved the dominant connection Andrew offered, and which Cam couldn't provide. The terror at losing his lover to this man snaked through his gut, slithering toward his heart. He closed his eyes, trying to imagine a life without Ethan. Never seeing those crystalline blue eyes sparkling with joy, never again tasting those lips or feeling the heat as that hard, perfect cock pressed its way into him...

He pulled away from Andrew, wrapping his arms around himself. As much as he believed Ethan loved him, there was no getting around the fact Cam could never offer Ethan what Andrew could.

"Hey," Andrew said softly. "Come back. Please." He touched Cam's back with his fingertips but Cam lay still, staring into the darkness. Gently, Andrew stroked his skin and despite himself Cam felt calmed, and aroused, by his touch.

Finally, in a small voice, Cam confessed, "I don't want to lose him. But I know I can't ever give him all that he needs. By definition, I can never be enough for him."

"And what about you, Cam? Don't you need what only a Dom can give you? Are the games you've been playing really enough to feed your soul? Don't you long to surrender yourself completely to someone who would cherish that gift?"

Andrew's words penetrated Cam's mind like tiny, piercing darts, all at once popping the façade he'd maintained for so many years. After Bryan, he'd convinced himself the BDSM play was enough—a way to scratch an itch without digging too deep for comfort. He'd been using the club scene as a substitute for what he really needed. Ethan had understood what Cam had tried to deny. Playing wasn't enough. It had to be real. The submission, the erotic exchange of power, for it to really matter, had to be authentic.

Lying there beside Andrew, he felt exposed and raw. Andrew was right. He longed to submit in the full sense of the word—to give himself, without hesitation or reservation, to a man who understood his longing and could quench its fire. He wanted a Dom who was also a lover. He wanted someone who could make him fly the way Andrew had, someone who could make his heart pound and his breath catch. Someone he could trust the way he trusted Ethan. Someone he could love. These thoughts swirled in his head but he gave voice to none of them, instead blurting, "But what about Ethan?"

"Ethan loves you. Anyone can see that just by looking at him when he looks at you. I'm not asking you to give up that love. What I'm trying to say, Cam, is I don't want to take him from you. Or you from him, for that matter. I want you both. I want to be the connection, the conduit that brings the two of you full circle. I think I can provide what's missing between you. If you let me."

Slowly Cam rolled back toward Andrew, staring with wonder at his silhouette in dark. His heart was beating fast and even though he was lying down he felt lightheaded. He had a sudden nearly desperate urge to feel skin on skin. Sitting up, he pulled his T-shirt over his head.

"Just our shirts. Would that be okay?"

"Sure." Andrew took off his own shirt and they lay back down, Cam resting his cheek against Andrew's warm, firm chest. It seemed so natural to lift his face. Andrew leaned toward him until their lips touched. The kiss was sweet, almost chaste.

Cam parted his lips but Andrew pulled back.

"Sleep now," he whispered, gathering Cam again into his arms.

chapter 14

ETHAN WAS BONE-tired but glad to be home. The dinner with their Japanese clients had gone well, and they were checked into their hotel by midnight. He had called Cam, but he hadn't picked up, not that he'd really expected him to. They were probably still at Samurai's party.

At the hotel, Ethan had fallen asleep for a couple of hours, only to come wide awake at three in the morning. He decided, rather than tossing and turning, he'd just head on back to New York. Roger, who was staying on for the weekend in Boston with friends, had given him Friday off, so he could catch up on his sleep once he got home.

He had showered and checked out, taking a cab to the South Station. The next train wasn't until 5:10, so he got some coffee and a paper and settled down on a bench. He tried to focus on the headlines, pushing away the images of Cam, naked and spread taut in front of a group of gaping onlookers while Andrew whipped him for the crowd, that kept insinuating themselves into his brain. It was good they were together, he told himself over and over. It would give them a chance to connect, without using him as the focal point.

Ethan tried to be quiet as he unlocked the apartment door. It was already after nine and Cam was usually at his shop by eight, but he might have slept in. Ethan wasn't expected back till at least noon. He smiled at the idea of surprising his sleeping lover with his early return.

Walking into the bedroom, he dropped his overnight bag on the floor. The bed was empty and neatly made. "Cam?" he called out, just in case, but no one answered. Ethan pulled out his cell, thinking to call Cam, but decided instead just to walk over the gallery and surprise him. He would stop at their favorite bakery and pick up some of the cheese Danish Cam loved.

When he arrived at the gallery the "Closed" sign was still on the front door and it was dark inside. Cam didn't usually open the gallery until ten, so maybe he was in the back shop, working.

Using his key, Ethan unlocked the door and checked the alarm pad. The alarm was still set. He disarmed it and stood in the center of the gallery, confused. Maybe Cam had gone to run an errand. Or get something to eat. Yes, that must be it.

Ethan pulled out his cell and pushed the speed dial for Cam. It went straight to voicemail. "Cam, It's me. I'm back in New York. Call me when you get this."

When Cam didn't call back after ten minutes or so, a slight niggling worry entered Ethan's mind. Cam had said he was going to drive into the city and pick Andrew up on the way to party. Cam wasn't the greatest driver to begin with, and New York traffic could be a bitch. He decided to take a walk over to the garage where he kept the car to make sure it was there and in one piece.

While he waited for the attendant to bring the car down, he tried Cam's cell phone one more time, but clicked off when it went again to voicemail, too agitated to leave another message.

"Sorry, Mr. Townsend," the attendant said, handing the keys back to him. "Your car isn't in. It was checked out yesterday evening and hasn't been brought back yet."

An unwelcome thought slipped into his mind. Could Cam still be at Andrew's? Trying hard not to leap to conclusions, Ethan called Andrew. No answer. He left a brief message. "Andrew. It's Ethan. Call me." He knew he'd sounded less than sub-like with his terse message, but he couldn't help it.

All his earlier fatigue had dropped away, replaced by a jittery edginess. Though he hadn't eaten since the night before, the thought of food turned his stomach. He tossed the bag of pastries into the trashcan on the street corner.

Descending into a subway tunnel, he waited for the train to Manhattan, trying not to imagine the worst. It didn't work. What bitter irony—here he'd practically thrust his lover and his Dom together, hoping it would make Cam more amenable to Andrew's having a place in their lives, and the plan had worked with a vengeance.

He couldn't stop the image of Cam on his hands and knees, looking back with adoration as Andrew penetrated him. *Stop it. You don't know anything. Don't leap to conclusions. Cam loves you. You love him. You can trust him.*

A young man in a faded T-shirt and dirty jeans sat across from Ethan, his hair the same rich auburn as Cam's, though it hung straight and lank, unlike Cam's unruly curls. As if feeling Ethan's eyes on him, the guy looked up, startling Ethan with same emerald green eyes, though they were deeper set and lacked the sparkle of Cam's eyes.

The first time they met was at Club de Sade, a BDSM club in the Village. Ethan had been there with Simon, a Dom friend of his and sometimes lover. They'd come to see a demonstration on the proper technique when using a bullwhip. Cam had been the volunteer on the small, raised stage that night.

It was the summer before this one and it had been a hot, muggy night. The basement club had no air conditioning and the air felt damp and thick. At first a squat, heavyset man with graying hair lectured about proper wrist technique, demonstrating with cracking flicks of the whip that made Ethan flinch.

Then the man, Ethan had forgotten his name now, called Cam to the stage. Cam was wearing a white T-shirt and cut-off blue jean shorts. With casual ease, he stripped down to his thong underwear, the sheer fabric leaving very little to the imagination in front and completely revealing his sexy ass.

He stood in profile to the audience, his skin pale in the stage light, his muscles lean and sharply defined. The tiny gold hoops at his nipples glinted in the stage light. His hair was even longer then, touching his shoulders when he let his head fall back, which he did, eyes closed in masochistic bliss as the tip of the formidable whip made contact.

From the beginning Ethan had had an immediate connection with Cam that went beyond mere physical attraction. He could almost feel the cut of that whip each time Cam winced. The man using the whip was of no consequence and Simon, too, faded from Ethan's consciousness. Nothing and no one existed that night except Cam on the stage, resplendent in his erotic submission, and Ethan, watching with aching desire.

When the demonstration was over, Cam turned toward the small audience with flushed cheeks and bright eyes. Ethan couldn't take his eyes off him. He felt as if he were perched on a high cliff, arms overhead, poised for a perfect dive. He'd been waiting on that cliff a long time, seeking the right man but never quite finding the courage or desire to leave the earth. When their eyes met, he took the leap, and he'd been falling ever since.

As the train hurtled toward Brooklyn, Ethan tried not to imagine the love of his life wrapped in another man's arms.

He failed.

~*~

Andrew lay in bed beside the sleeping Cam, drifting pleasantly in and out of consciousness. He could hear the vibrating buzz of his cell phone in the other room but was too comfortable to get up and see who it was. They could leave a message.

He'd already arranged to take Friday off. He knew he should probably wake Cam and send him on his way, but he made no move to do so. He'd fallen half in love last night. There was a sweetness to Cam, an innocence that was wildly appealing.

He rolled toward Cam, coming up on an elbow to gaze down at the sleeping man, and for the first time the thought that he'd rather be with Ethan didn't enter his mind. Or rather, it did, but when he examined it, he realized it was no longer true. What he really wanted was for Ethan to be asleep on his other side.

He wanted a meaningful relationship. He wanted something real. He wanted it with Ethan and Cam. He knew they wanted what he offered as a Dom, but was there room in their lives for another lover? Was it possible for three people to be lovers, equal in that love, or would someone always feel left out?

Because of the unique quality of a D/s relationship, he actually thought it might work, in theory. If they would have him, he would love the chance to try it in practice. As their Dom, Andrew was confident he could control any petty jealousies that might erupt between the guys. He would work hard to make sure both of them felt loved and cherished. He could keep them both on that delicious edge of erotic submission, too on fire to worry about who loved whom more or less.

The intercom buzzed, startling Andrew. Cam didn't move. Andrew rolled from the bed and stumbled toward the front door, wondering who was there. He pushed the button. "Yes?"

"Andrew. It's Ethan. Is Cam there?"

"Ethan! I thought you were still in Boston."

"Answer my question." He could hear the steel in Ethan's tone.

"Yes, he's—"

"Let me in. Now." The guy had obviously jumped to a whole lot of conclusions, not all of them incorrect.

"Ethan, calm down. It's not what—"

"Let me in."

Andrew pressed the button to release the lobby door lock. He hurried to the bedroom. "Cam, wake up. Ethan's here."

"Mmm?" Cam answered sleepily. Andrew moved to the bed and shook Cam's shoulder. "Get up. Ethan's on his way up right now."

Cam sat up abruptly, his eyes wide. "Ethan? Here?"

"Yeah."

"Shit, what time is it?"

"It's ten-thirty."

"Fuck," Cam said. He jumped from the bed. "Where's my shirt?"

"Here, you can wear this." Andrew tossed him a T-shirt and pulled on one himself. There was a knock at the door, or rather, a pounding.

Andrew went to door, which he unlocked and pulled open. Ethan burst over the threshold. "Where is he?" he demanded, pushing past Andrew, his eyes darting around the room.

"Ethan, stop it." Andrew put a hand on Ethan's shoulder but he shook it off. Cam appeared, his curls tousled, his face still marked with sleep.

"Ethan." Cam smiled, moving toward them. Ethan gave him a stony look and Cam's smile fell away. "What's wrong?"

"What *wrong*? I can't believe this. I go out of town for one night and this happens."

"*What* happens?" Cam shot back, crossing his arms over his chest. Andrew had been about to say the same thing, but held his tongue.

Ethan stared at his lover and shook his head, an expression of disbelief washing over his face. "Don't play the wounded innocent, Cameron McNamee. Not when the evidence is staring me in the face." He waved his arm around the living room, as if pictures of Cam and Andrew naked and having sex were plastered on the walls.

"I come home to an empty house. Your shop is closed. You don't answer your cell. Neither does Andrew. I come here to find you obviously having just woken up. What kind of a fool do you take me for?"

Cam narrowed his green eyes and when he spoke, his voice was quiet but cutting. "Whatever you think happened here, did it occur to you to *ask*? Or did you just assume we'd lie to cover up whatever is going on behind your back? Is this what you think of me? Of Andrew? Shit, Ethan, you're the one who practically forced me to go to the party! Yeah, I wanted to go, but it didn't even occur to me to go without you. Not until you insisted. When I questioned you, you said you trusted me."

Cam's voice rose. "And all that talk about trust before. Was that just so much bullshit so you could get what you wanted? That lecture about me trusting us as a couple if we were to get more involved with Andrew, was that just so you could be with him? Is that what this is really about, Ethan? You're jealous because you think all you shared behind my back was a kiss, while I got to fuck the guy?"

Ethan flushed a dark red. "So you admit it."

"No, I don't fucking admit anything, you dope! I'm trying to get into that crazy head of yours!"

"Well, what the hell am I supposed to think?" Ethan sputtered. "My lover spends the night with my Dom. You can't deny that. I caught you red-handed. You couldn't even be bothered to put back on your own fucking clothes! How much more obvious did you want to make it, for crying out loud?"

"Oh, so he's *your* Dom now. All that crap you spouted about bringing Andrew into *our* lives was really just a cover to sanction you having your cake and eating it too."

"Don't try to change the subject." Ethan pointed an accusing finger at Cam. "Where'd you get that T-shirt? I've never seen that shirt before. You've obviously been here all fucking night. Or should I say all night *fucking.*"

Cam glanced down at the shirt Andrew had tossed him. Larger than his own shirts, it hung loosely over his slender frame. The shirt was a faded red with the words, "Normal people scare me," in white. He opened his mouth to protest but Andrew got there first.

"Ethan, that's *enough.* And Cam, calm down. Ethan's overreacting because he doesn't know what's going on. I want both of you to be quiet and take a deep breath."

He waited, not at all sure they would obey. They were both looking at him now, Cam scowling, Ethan's eyes burning with righteous indignation.

"Okay," Andrew said after a few beats. "We're going to sit down, all three of us, and talk this out. No secrets, no accusations, okay?" Cam nodded. Ethan said nothing, but he did follow the other two to the couches. Andrew sat opposite the pair and leaned forward, aware this was a pivotal moment in the fledgling relationship between three.

He looked at Ethan, his heart skipping a beat as those brilliant blue eyes stared into his. "*Nothing* happened last night. *Your* lover and *your* Dom," Andrew couldn't stop the trace of a smile that rose to his lips as he quoted Ethan's use of the possessive, "did *not* fuck each other behind your back. We went to the party. We shared a scene. Cam had too much to drink so I drove him here. He spent the night. We did not have sex. Got it?"

Ethan's hands were clenched into fists on his lap. His head swiveled toward Cam to Andrew and back again to Cam. "You expect me to believe that?"

"I expect no less, Ethan," Andrew replied quietly.

Cam put his hand over one of Ethan's closed fists. Suddenly it was as if Ethan were a balloon and someone had just let the air out. He slumped back against the sofa.

Andrew leaned forward. "Ethan, when I first reconnected with you, I had fantasies about stealing you away from your lover and making you my own, I won't deny it. And as I've gotten to know you, really know you, not just the fantasy from all those years ago, but the real man, the desire to make you my own has gotten even stronger. But along with that, I've come to know and desire Cam as well.

"It was good that Cam and I had some time alone." Ethan's expression darkened. Andrew held out a hand and shook his head. "No, stop it. You need to let that go, Ethan. If two are to become three, there's no room for that kind of jealousy."

Andrew paused, aware his heart was beating uncomfortably fast. He waited for one or both to deny they wanted anything more than a casual play partner. Neither spoke, so he plunged on. "What I mean is, it was a chance for us to connect on our own. If this is going to work, we need that dynamic. It moves the relationship from a triangle to a circle, if you want to think about it that way—moving in an unbroken line instead jerking from one to the other, if you follow me."

"Yeah," Cam said softly. Ethan's fingers had relaxed. He turned over the hand on which Cam's hand was still resting and their fingers intertwined. Andrew's heart ached to be a part of that easy closeness, but at least he had Ethan's attention now. Both men were watching him, listening hard. He had the feeling he was auditioning for the role of his life. Taking a breath, he continued.

"I've loved what we've shared so far. I'm thirty-three and for the first time I've found not one, but two guys who I think I could spend my life, or at least the foreseeable future with. I've been thinking a lot about this. It's time to move to the next level. I want to be more than your part-time Dom. If the two of you will have me, I want to be your lover as well. Your partner, as well as your Dom.

"But I'm not an idiot. I'm aware you've been together a year. I'm not demanding that you love me—obviously that's not something that can be demanded. I just want to know if you think the three of us could move to something higher, something more meaningful than weekend dungeon scenes."

Aware he was talking too much, Andrew cut to the chase. "Here's my proposal. One week. My place has plenty of room. You guys agree to stay here, starting tonight. We have the weekend and then during the week, we work as usual but spend our nights together. Think of it as a trial run for what it would be like if I owned you 24/7. I'm not talking about collared slaves, I'm speaking in the metaphorical sense—the sensual exchange of power a sub willingly offers his Dom. The acceptance of your submission on a fulltime basis.

"For this week, you would both be expected to serve me at my pleasure when we're together here. I would expect your complete submission and devotion and in turn offer you the experience and control you both need and crave. Of course, certain ground rules would be in effect—while under my roof you would be subject to my dictates, but I'm sure, as the true submissives I know you both to be, you wouldn't have it any other way."

He stood, speaking quickly to keep either guy from responding. "Please, don't say anything yet. I know I just threw a lot at you. I'm going to go down to a little deli I like and get us some breakfast, okay? I want to give you some time alone to talk this over. And please understand—this isn't an ultimatum or anything like that. If you guys think it's best to stay at this level, I'm willing, for a while. You both have come to mean too much to me to make this an all or nothing thing. Just understand I've come to a realization since I've met you. I want a different kind of life. For the first time, I don't just want to take—I want to give."

~*~

The front door closed with a click. They were both silent for several beats. In a way Cam was glad Andrew had absented himself, though it was kind of strange to be sitting with Ethan in his apartment, without him there.

He was still trying to get his head around what Andrew had just said. Last night had felt so good, so *right*. He finally admitted with a dawning wonder that he'd had a hole in his life since Bryan, no, even with Bryan. He needed a Dom as much as Ethan did. It wasn't just an itch, it was a basic part of the fabric of who he was.

At the same time, he remained annoyed, even angry, with Ethan, for leaping to the conclusion he'd fucked the guy the minute Ethan's back was turned. Some of his anger must have showed in his face because Ethan reached for him, contrition etched in his features.

"Hey," Ethan said softly. "I'm sorry I was such a jerk just now. I got scared when I came home and you were no place around and didn't answer your phone. I think I let my imagination get the best of me. The thought of losing you to him or—" Ethan bit his lip and Cam knew with absolute certainty what he'd been about to say.

"...Or him to me," he supplied. "You don't want to lose Andrew."

"Oh, Cam." There was anguish in Ethan's voice, but he didn't deny it. "It's you I love, you know that." Conviction entered his voice. "If you want us to break it off with Andrew right now, say the word. It's done."

Cam was quiet, weighing Ethan's words. Was he sincere? And if they ended things, could they really return to the artificial arrangement they'd concocted—giving their bodies and their submission to strangers on weekends, while saving their hearts for each other?

He wasn't at all sure that was possible anymore. Like it or not, Andrew had torn the fabric of that arrangement so completely, he doubted it could be repaired. But he realized he didn't want to repair it—he was ready to move forward to something new. He craved what Andrew offered, but more than that, he was forced to admit he wanted not only the experience, but the man himself.

Did that mean he loved Ethan less?

Ethan was watching him, those diamond eyes filled with such raw love the last vestige of Cam's anger fell away. He took Ethan's hands in his. "I don't want that. I know you don't either. Look, this is new for us. It's a strange situation to be in. But it's exciting too. Being with Andrew has made me realize some things. I think I was in denial about how negatively my experience with Bryan colored my perception of the scene. Instead of looking for the right guy, I took the easy way out, keeping it superficial to protect myself. I think," he paused, hoping Ethan would understand this didn't mean he loved Ethan less, "I think I'm ready for more. For something real."

"So you think we should do this? This week thing?"

"What about you?" Cam waited. He did want it, but only if Ethan did too. When Ethan didn't respond right away, Cam prodded gently, "What is it you're afraid of? Do you still think something happened between me and Andrew last night?"

"No, no, it's not that. I mean, I do think something happened, but not sex."

"What?"

"You connected. You feel the same powerful draw that I do." Cam nodded, waiting.

"What if…?" Ethan trailed off.

"What if what?"

"What if you fall in love with him?"

Cam shook his head emphatically. "You mean *instead* of you? Oh, Ethan, never. No way. Not happening." He pulled his lover into his arms and they kissed for a long, passionate moment.

When they fell apart, Cam said, "And what about you? You're more than a little in love with the guy. Will there be room in *your* heart for two?"

"In love with Andrew? Me?" Ethan stared at Cam, as if this were a revelation. Finally, he nodded with a kind of wonderment. "Yeah," he said in a whisper. "I guess I am."

"Well, guess what? So am I."

chapter 15

"DON'T DO IT, Ethan. He said not to."

"I know, I know." Ethan's cock was throbbing. He put his hands behind his head and stared up at the ceiling. He hadn't come for several days. That in itself wouldn't have been so bad, but Andrew had spent over an hour alternating between stroking their cocks nearly to orgasm and engaging in the most exquisite cock and ball torture.

They'd returned to his place that evening with packed bags, both nervous and excited by what they had agreed to do. Over pizza, the three of them had discussed their medical histories. Andrew had provided proof of his whistle-clean bill of health, and they had done the same. It was a slightly awkward but necessary ritual for sexually active men that all three of them appreciated. They'd gone on to talk about their expectations and limits for the week ahead.

After dinner, Andrew had them shower and shave their pubic areas smooth, which had the effect of making Ethan feel especially vulnerable, no doubt Andrew's intent. Both pleasure and pain were heightened on bare, smooth flesh.

"Please, Sir," he'd gasped, more than once during the erotic play. "I'm going to—"

"No, you're not," Andrew had snapped, dropping Ethan's cock and gripping his balls hard. "You'll come when I tell you to. Not before. This week I take your measure, Ethan Wise. From what I've learned so far, you can handle pain with considerable grace but you're a slut. You're focused too much on your own pleasure. I'll teach you to control that impulse. It's high time you learned."

It was true and he knew it. Cam was much better at controlling himself. Andrew brought him to the edge as well, while Ethan watched with hungry eyes. But Cam never begged or shuddered with repressed need. He would close his eyes, breathing deeply, forcing back his climax in an act of sheer will.

Andrew had sent them to bed early and by all accounts Ethan should have passed out. He was operating on very little sleep, having barely slept the night before in the Boston hotel room. But his damn cock refused to behave. It jutted hard against his belly, aching to be touched.

Ethan wasn't crazy about the sleeping arrangements. He and Cam were each in their own twin bed, though at least they shared a room. Ethan had envisioned the three of them sleeping together in Andrew's king-size bed. In his vision he had been the one in the middle, happily spooned between his two lovers.

But Andrew had other ideas. "You will earn privileges as the week progresses, based on your progress. Sleeping in your Master's bed is not something you earn lightly. Be glad I'm allowing you in a bed at all. I considered having you sleep on the floor."

They'd been in bed for nearly an hour already, whispering about the day's events and what to expect tomorrow. It was exciting to be there, in Andrew's house, with Cam fully onboard. It was the chance of a lifetime for them both—the chance to make a truly meaningful connection with a Dom, while still keeping their own special relationship.

Andrew had warned they would be up early—he wanted to take full advantage of the weekend. If only Ethan's damn cock would go to sleep, then he could get some rest. The light shining from the hallway didn't help. He wanted to get up and close the door, but he didn't dare.

When they'd discussed the house rules for the week to come, along with never orgasming without express permission, no doors were ever to be closed to Andrew, not even the bathroom door. It was, he told them, just another small way to remind them they belonged to him.

"Cam," Ethan whispered. "You awake?" Cam didn't reply, his breathing now slow and steady. Ethan shifted on the small mattress, rolling from his side to his back. His stiff cock tented the sheet. Unable to help himself, he reached for it, stroking it for a few seconds.

Oh, it felt so good. Just a little more. He wouldn't come. He'd just rub it a little to ease the pressure. His other hand joined the first, cupping his balls. In his mind's eye he saw Andrew standing in front of Cam, whose shaven cock and balls jutted out invitingly from his body.

Earlier that night in the dungeon, Andrew had placed a series of heavy metal rings around Cam's balls and along the length of his shaft. From these he'd hung lead weights shaped like teardrops.

Using a small rubber whip he called the stinger, he'd flicked it at Cam's cock and balls, making him wince. Cam was bound to the cross, his arms spread wide, his ankles secured in sturdy cuffs. When he closed his eyes, Andrew moved closer. "Open your eyes. Keep them open and look at me."

Ethan could almost feel each stinging cut of the whip, one of the tails of which was about an inch longer than the rest. It was that bit of rubber that made Cam wince like that.

Ethan knew this well, as Andrew had treated him to the same erotic torture only minutes before. He, too, was secured, though in the cock stocks, his cock and balls compressed between the wooden slats of his prison. He'd nearly come at least six times.

But this time Andrew wasn't there to stop him. Cam, the voice of conscience, was sleeping. Who would know if he stole just one orgasm? Just one, to take the edge off, so he could sleep and be refreshed and ready to start the morning with a clean slate.

It felt good. So good. Just a few more strokes, just a few...

Ethan groaned involuntarily as he ejaculated beneath the sheets. A moment later the light came on overhead. Andrew strode into the room, moving so quickly he was beside Ethan before Ethan realized what was happening.

Grabbing the sheet, Andrew jerked it back. The telltale evidence was spread on Ethan's stomach and chest. Andrew eyed Ethan's body with a stern look and Ethan knew he was blushing a hot red.

"Andrew! How did you know—I mean, I'm sorry, I—"

"Not a word." Andrew cut him off. He pointed to the ground. "Kneel at attention on the floor. Don't move till I get back."

Ethan bit his lip to keep from speaking. He wanted to beg, to make excuses, to apologize, but the look in Andrew's face, along with his command not to speak, kept Ethan silent. Miserably he rolled from the bed and assumed the ordered position, kneeling up with a straight back, eyes ahead, hands resting palms up on his thighs. The semen dribbled its way down his stomach but he didn't dare to wipe it away.

"What happened?" Cam asked sleepily, leaning up an elbow and squinting in the bright light.

The blush was still hot on Ethan's face. He didn't answer. Cam looked at him, his eyes widening as he took in situation. "Ethan. You didn't." He shook his head and Ethan looked away, now thoroughly humiliated in front of his lover.

For an instant he considered just getting up and walking out. It wasn't as if Andrew actually owned him, for crying out loud. He was his own man. If he wanted to jerk off, that was his prerogative. Who the hell was Andrew to dictate when he came or didn't come?

The rebellious moment passed as quickly as it had come. Who was Andrew? The first man Ethan had felt truly submissive toward, that's who. The first man he thought he might actually want to be with, along with Cam by his side.

If nothing else, he owed it to *himself* to give this week his best shot. The BDSM play at the clubs was no longer enough. He wanted what Andrew offered. So why had he blown it right out of the gate? Even if Andrew hadn't caught him, he'd been cheating. He'd cheapened the potential of their submissive experience by willfully violating his Dom's express dictates.

How the heck had Andrew known what he was doing? Was he lurking outside the door, just waiting to catch him? If only he could undo the last fifteen minutes and start over. He was the one who claimed he wanted this real, so why had he snuck around like a teenaged idiot? Along with chagrin and embarrassment, real remorse washed over Ethan. When Andrew returned a moment later, he whispered a heartfelt, "I'm sorry, Sir."

Maybe it was the sincerity in his tone or the expression on his face. Whatever it was, Andrew's stern visage eased a little and a hint of a smile seemed to brush his lips. "Next time you jerk off without permission, maybe you should bite your pillow or something. Your moan carried clear into my room. It wasn't too hard to figure out what the hell was going on in here."

He held up a thick strap of leather with cuffs on either side. "Since you aren't yet capable of resisting temptation, we'll just remove the temptation. Stand up and lift your arms overhead."

Ethan stood quickly, hoping somehow to redeem himself. Andrew secured the belt around his waist and buckled it in place at his back. "Put your wrists in the cuffs," he said. Ethan did so and Andrew clipped them shut, snapping the small padlocks into place. Andrew dabbed at the gooey ejaculate with a tissue, shaking his head.

He pushed lightly against Ethan's shoulder. "Now go to bed. We'll discuss your punishment in the morning."

~*~

They were again in the dungeon, Ethan still in his bondage belt, his nose pressed into a corner, a butt plug in his ass for good measure. Andrew had left Ethan to spend the night in the cuffs. Cam had wanted to go over to him once Andrew had left the bedroom, to offer his lover some comfort. But Andrew had explicitly forbid him from either getting out of his bed or talking to Ethan.

Ethan's punishment was the worst sort in Cam's submissive mind—that of being totally ignored. He felt sorry for Ethan, but, even though it was Ethan's first 24/7 experience, he silently agreed with Andrew that punishment was definitely in order for such a flagrant violation of expressly stated rules.

Even at breakfast Andrew had left Ethan in his cuffs, feeding him scrambled eggs and bits of bacon from his own plate and holding the orange juice to his lips. "Until I'm sure you can keep your hands where they belong," he'd admonished in a teasing tone, "they'll stay in their cuffs."

When Andrew had stepped away a moment to pour himself another mug of coffee, Cam caught Ethan's eye. Silently he mouthed, "You okay?"

Ethan nodded and, on an impulse, Cam glanced beneath the table. Unlike Cam, who had been permitted to put on a pair of shorts for breakfast, Ethan had remained naked. Despite his predicament, or perhaps because of it, Cam saw his erection jutting stiffly beneath the table. He grinned at Ethan, who grinned back, if a little shamefacedly.

Now Andrew said, "Lie down on the bondage table. I'm going to show you what was missing the other night during Jermaine's little scene."

Cam lay on the table, allowing Andrew to push his legs up, feet flat, until his heels were touching his ass. He had already placed cuffs on Cam's wrists after he'd had him strip. Using a piece of rope, he secured the cuffs to a sturdy hook embedded in the wall at the head of the bondage table, pulling Cam's arms taut.

"You're already good at orgasm control. And I'm not interested in denying you that particular pleasure. That's not what this about. I'm going to do what Jermaine did, but you'll see how very different the experience can be."

"Yes, Sir." Cam swallowed nervously. Bryan had milked him on occasion, using a tool similar to the ones Jermaine had used on his slave boys. Cam had submitted to it, but had never really liked it. Bryan had done it as punishment, draining Cam's seminal fluid without the accompanying pleasure of orgasm, much as Jermaine had done during the scene.

Andrew stood over him, stroking his chest and legs in long, fluid movements. "Relax. I can feel your tension. Trust me. That's part of this lesson. The only true submission can come when there is complete trust between partners. I don't expect you to have that yet—we're too new.

"I was watching you during the milking scene at the party. You had a lot of trouble with it. I want to show you it doesn't have to be like that. It can be a very sensual experience."

"Yes, Sir," Cam said again, not believing him.

Andrew continued to stroke Cam's body, massaging his arms, legs and torso, touching everything except Cam's cock, which rose, nevertheless, in anticipation. Taking a small tube from his pants pocket, Andrew squirted some lubricant onto his fingers. Placing his other hand firmly on Cam's chest, directly over his heart, he pressed the lubed fingers gently against Cam's small, puckered hole.

He moved his fingers slowly, carefully easing them inside. It felt good, as did Andrew's hand on his chest. Cam closed his eyes and sighed. "Open your eyes," Andrew said. "Look at me. Keep your eyes on my face, no matter what I'm doing to do you. Do you understand?"

"Yes, Sir," Cam murmured, fixing his gaze on Andrew's coppery brown eyes, drawn to the spark of fire in his stare.

Andrew slid his fingers in, moving them up and back until he found what he was looking for. Cam let out a small, involuntary cry as a tingly sensation pervaded his loins, not unlike the feeling just before orgasm.

Andrew smiled. "Yes. I've found it. Keep your eyes on mine. Relax. Trust me. Trust yourself." Gently, he massaged Cam's prostate through the delicate membrane that separated it from the rectum. Several times Cam found his eyes beginning to close. He forced himself to focus and concentrate as Andrew had directed.

His cock was hard, pointing upward against his stomach. He felt the warm drizzle of semen begin to issue from it as Andrew continued the internal massage. Andrew wrapped his free hand around Cam's cock, sliding his thumb over the head of the crown and pressing against the slit.

The sensation was different from when Bryan had used the milking tool, thrusting it inside Cam and forcing the semen from him, without otherwise touching him. Andrew was staring into his eyes, his fingers moving inside Cam's most intimate place, his other hand gently stroking the leaking shaft.

Instead of the gushing spurt of an actual orgasm, it was more like a prolonged, if less intense, climax. "Good, yes. That's it," Andrew crooned, moving his fingers gently inside of Cam while Cam's milky semen trickled over his other hand.

He wanted Andrew to bend down and kiss him. Or better yet, he wanted Ethan there behind his head, a witness, a partner in this. He pretended Ethan was there, instead of cuffed with his nose in a corner.

They would get there, he told himself. The three of them would find their rhythm.

Andrew stroked his cock and ran his fingers lightly over Cam's sac, while still massaging him from within. Cam's eyes closed again despite his best intentions, caught in the powerful grip of an endless, if gentle, climax.

He didn't know how long it went on, Andrew relentlessly pulling pleasure from him in a slow, steady tingle. At last the hands were withdrawn. Cam lay limp, drifting in a sensual lassitude. He was aware when Andrew walked away and then, after some moments, returned.

"Cam."

Slowly Cam opened his eyes. Andrew touched the back of his hand to Cam's lips and instinctively he kissed it. He found he couldn't stop kissing it, a wave of submissive gratitude suddenly overwhelming him. If his hands had been free, he would have used them to keep that hand at his mouth, so he could kiss it over and over.

Andrew took the hand away, but he was smiling.

"Thank you, Sir," Cam breathed. "That was amazing. I've never experienced anything like that before."

"You're welcome. It wouldn't have happened like that without trust. So thank you, too, Cam."

He untied Cam's cuffs from the wall and helped him to sit up on the table. Turning toward poor Ethan, nose still in the corner, he said, "I think he's been punished enough, don't you?"

"Yes, Sir." Cam grinned, and together they went to rescue Ethan, who, Cam was sure, had learned his lesson.

~*~

Andrew looked at the glowing green numbers on his digital clock for the hundredth time. 1:48 A.M. He needed to get to sleep—he had in important meeting first thing the next morning—but he couldn't seem to shut off his racing mind.

He closed his eyes and took several deep, calming breaths. The week was nearly over and he couldn't deny each sub had outdone himself in his sincere effort to earn Andrew's approval. After Ethan's initial disobedience, he'd redoubled his efforts to be the model sub. They'd both submitted with grace and passion to every erotic torture and pleasure Andrew could devise.

Ethan could take a significant amount of pain, transcending it after an initial struggle and getting to that submissive place of utter peace that Andrew both admired and envied. Cam's threshold of pain was lower, but his self-control was greater than Ethan's. It was a challenge to see how far he could take Cam with orgasm denial and control.

He enjoyed using both subs at once, setting up playful competitions, like when he had them take turns sucking each other's cock, timing them to see who could hold out the longest, then "punishing" the one who came first.

Andrew looked at the clock again. Four minutes had passed. Maybe if he could wrap his arms around the two sexy guys he'd consigned to the twin beds in the guest room, he'd be able to relax and drift into peaceful dreams.

Why didn't he just go get them and have them climb in with him? He was the Dom, wasn't he? He was the one who had pompously announced they would have to "earn" their way into his bed. Hadn't they earned it in spades?

But that wasn't really what it was about, was it? At least not entirely. Behind the façade of training them during this probationary week, Andrew was afraid. When he'd invited them to spend a week with him, it had sounded great in the abstract. They would move beyond the superficial BDSM of the club games and explore a meaningful D/s relationship.

From the start he'd admitted to himself he was in love with Ethan, and as the days passed, Cam was quickly taking his place beside Ethan in his heart. That was a good thing, right?

Yeah, but it was a terrifying thing too. To love was to leave oneself vulnerable, something Andrew wasn't used to doing.

He'd never felt this open, this exposed, and it scared the crap out of him. It wasn't that he didn't think he was capable of love, or of being loved. It was the fact that Ethan and Cam were a couple. They'd been together a year before he even arrived on the scene. How could he hope to compete with such a preexisting connection?

Once Monday had rolled around, they had spent their days apart, working at their jobs, reconnecting in the evening at his apartment. He was usually the last to arrive, and he would find them naked and kneeling by his front door, heads touching the floor, holding hands.

It was that holding of the hands that was his undoing. That constant reminder they were lovers first, his submissives second. He wanted more. This week had shown him the potential of a different kind of life. He saw with painful clarity how long he'd been alone, by choice, because of fear.

He knew he was still operating off that fear now, still keeping them at arm's length by not allowing them into his bed at night. They'd talked through their experience every night at dinner, and both Ethan and Cam had been shiny-eyed and eager to continue, each asserting it had been the most exciting, fulfilling week of their lives.

He was the one who was keeping them away. He was the one who was holding back. He had asked, even demanded, that his subs hold back nothing—giving him their devotion, their submission, their hearts and minds. How could he ask that, if he weren't prepared to give the same in return?

chapter 16

TONIGHT WAS THE night.

He was going to put his heart on the line and offer himself, not Dom to sub, but man to man. After the session he would offer the gifts he'd had specially made earlier that week. After that, it was up to them.

He was distracted from his musings by his handsome subs tethered and kneeling before him, waiting for the erotic torture they knew was sure to come. They were kneeling up, facing each other, their fingers interlaced behind their necks, their cocks tethered together by braided nylon rope that criss-crossed and encircled the lengths of their shafts.

Andrew had bound each cock in a sort of Chinese finger trap made of cord. Then he'd attached the excess cord between the two to each other, so that when Cam moved, it pulled on Ethan's cock, and vice versa. For good measure, he'd attached a black metal ball collar around each sub's scrotum, adding a shiny round red weight to each, which swayed like miniature Christmas ornaments between their legs.

"Ethan," Andrew commanded. "Lean back." He watched as Ethan cautiously leaned backwards, pulling Cam's cock taut and making the heavy weight tugging at his balls sway on its short chain. "More," Andrew ordered. Ethan leaned back farther until Cam groaned, squeezing his eyes shut.

"Back in position. Now you, Cam. Give him as good as he gave you." Cam obeyed with less hesitation, leaning backward until Ethan winced and drew in a sharp breath.

"Excellent," Andrew said, moving to stand in front of the two men. He slipped a black nylon sleep mask over each man's eyes. "Remember, the stiller you are, the less pain you'll cause your partner."

He started with the flogger, warming each man's ass, thighs and back with its tresses. Next he selected the rubber whip, its tips delivering more of a sting than the soft leather of the flogger. A particularly sharp blow to Cam's ass produced an involuntary jerk on his part that pulled Ethan forward by his cock.

"Ah," Ethan moaned, though his tethered shaft remained rock hard. Stripping off his shirt, Andrew danced around the two men, alternating between the rubber whip and a slapper of shiny leather that cracked against their flesh like a gun's report. He enjoyed their startled expressions when leather or rubber made contact, neither knowing where it would land or on whom.

He switched at last to the cane, watching both men flinch, no matter whose ass was marked by the cut of bamboo. He found himself falling into a kind of trance of his own, moving from man to man, breathing hard along with them, his cock straining with each sexy, breathy cry of erotic pain he wrenched from their lips.

When his own cock was too hard to carry on, Andrew dropped the toys and stood over the rope-bound cocks pulled parallel between his legs. Pulling open his jeans, he pulled out his cock and nudged the tip at Ethan's lips, which parted instantly. Ethan leaned forward, eagerly sucking at his Master's cock while Cam waited silently behind them. After a few minutes, he turned toward Cam, whose mouth opened just as eagerly, swallowing Andrew's cock to the hilt.

On an impulse, Andrew used one hand to hold Cam's head in place, the other to pinch his nostrils shut. Cam stayed perfectly still, the only evidence of the increasing lack of oxygen, the reddening of his neck. When Andrew gauged Cam couldn't take much more, he said, "Five more seconds. You can do it. For me."

Cam remained still as stone, though he'd begun to tremble. Andrew counted for him and then pulled back while Cam gasped for air. Well pleased, Andrew turned to Ethan. "Let's see how well you do with that little exercise."

He pushed the head of his cock into Ethan's mouth, moving forward until it was lodged in his throat. As he'd done with Cam, he pinched Ethan's nostrils, cutting off his airflow. "I control your very breath," he said, his cock throbbing in the wet heat of Ethan's mouth and throat.

Ethan didn't manage quite as well, trying to pull back after only forty seconds, compared to Cam's full minute or more. Aware he could safely keep him that way for at least another minute, Andrew continued to hold him fast. To Ethan's credit, he did manage to keep his arms in position behind his head and didn't struggle after the initial involuntary spasm.

"Five seconds," Andrew said. "You can do it." He counted and then let go, watching Ethan gulp for air like a drowning man. He allowed himself a grin that neither guy could see as he tucked his erection away.

He pulled the masks from their eyes and knelt beside them so the three of them were positioned in a triangle. First he removed the heavy weights that swayed beneath their ball sacs.

Tugging at the slipknots that bound their shafts, he quickly undid the ropes from each hard cock and released the hinged metal ball collars. Both men breathed sighs of relief.

A look passed between them, part excitement, part love and then, as if on cue, they both turned to him, eyes smiling along with their lips. "Thank you, Sir," they said, one after the other.

"You're welcome," Andrew answered. "So welcome." If only they knew how much he would welcome them into his life on a permanent basis.

So tell them.

The words slipped into his head as if someone outside of himself had spoken. Tell them. Tell them you want them to stay. Tell them you never realized what love could be. Tell them how powerful the D/s experience is when there's submission times two and love times three.

He felt the need to speak, to say these things aloud, move like a storm from deep in his gut. A column of wind rose into his mouth with the words he had to say, but when he opened it to speak, there was nothing left but air.

Maybe they saw something in his eyes. Maybe the invitation he longed to extend was written there for those who could read past his reticence. Ethan leaned forward first, closing his eyes and parting his lips.

It was so natural to meet him halfway, their lips connecting a slow burn that intensified as tongues twisted together. Ethan pulled away, only to be replaced by Cam, whose kiss was just as ardent. They wanted him. Him, Andrew Townsend, not just some Dom who fit their kink. He knew it then as surely as he'd ever known anything.

Happiness hurtled through him, its buoyancy pushing him to his feet. "I have something for you both. For all three of us, actually," he said, feeling at once excited and shy. "Get dressed and meet me in the bedroom."

He left the room, heading toward the living room, where he'd left his briefcase. He pulled out the three oblong jewelry boxes, one white, one black and one gray. Giving the guys time to dress, he went into the kitchen and got a bottle of cold water from the refrigerator, drinking most of it before heading to the bedroom.

Cam and Ethan were waiting side-by-side, now dressed in jeans and T-shirts, perched on the bed, each one more handsome than the other. Aware of the symbolism of his gesture, Andrew knelt before them. He well knew that the power he exerted over the two subs was completely voluntary and consensual. It was more than an erotic power exchange—it was a gift.

Feeling in a way like he was proposing, this feeling reinforced by being on his knees, Andrew said, "This is the last day of our trial week. I wanted to give you something to mark our time together, and hopefully more than that."

He handed Ethan the white box and Cam the black. "I had these made by an artist I know who works in leather," Andrew continued. He showed them the third box and lifting the lid said, "Go ahead, open them." He watched as Ethan and Cam took off the lids and lifted out the thin strips of soft, supple leather, each fitted with a silver clasp. Cam's was red, Ethan's blue and his own, purple.

"They're collars." He wound his in a loop around his wrist. "Though I, as your Dom, will wear mine at my wrist rather than my throat, I like the symbolic gesture of wearing it for you.

With it, I remind myself that a loving Dom belongs to his subs as much as they belong to him.

"If you choose to accept these," Andrew pushed on, ignoring his now pounding heart, "when at home, I will expect them to always be in place. When you're out, especially at work and other places where discretion is necessary, you can wear them as bracelets."

"It's beautiful," Cam said, running his finger over the buttery soft leather.

"You're asking us to be your collared slaves?" Ethan asked.

Andrew stood, looking down at the two men. "No. That is, I don't believe a Master/slave relationship is sustainable. Not in the real world. I'm asking for something more. I'm asking the two of you to give yourselves to me in body and spirit. To accept my dominance and offer your submission. To give me a chance to become a full partner in your lives, not just a weekend Dom, but a lover.

"We've known each other less than a month. I might be asking too much. But know this. If you choose to put on those collars, you will belong to me. As long as they are around your necks, you will serve me as I see fit. Your body, your orgasms, all sensual control, will belong to me. When we go about our daily lives, of course you're free to act as you see fit. But once you step over this threshold, you are mine."

Ethan and Cam looked at each other, their eyes soft. Not for the first time, it seemed to Andrew the two of them could communicate without speaking. He wondered if he'd ever reach that state of closeness with the two of them. Or was this the end, here and now? Had he pushed them too far, too fast?

He held his breath as he watched their silent exchange. They nodded to one another and then turned toward him, both slipping from the bed onto their knees.

"We want it," Cam said. "Very much."

"Yes," Ethan echoed. They held out their hands, the collars resting on their palms and bowed their heads. Understanding, Andrew took the collars and secured one around each man's neck, nearly dizzy with happiness and relief.

Once the collars were in place, he tapped each man on his shoulder and they rose, used to this silent command after their week in his care. "I want you." Andrew addressed them both, his voice a low growl. His cock was near to bursting. He tugged at the fly of his jeans and kicked out of them.

"Get naked and ready for me. I'm going to claim you." Cam and Ethan wasted no time stripping again. Andrew saw the faint welts on their asses from his cane and this just served to make his cock even harder.

"Cam, you sit at the head of the bed and spread your legs. Ethan's going to suck your cock while I fuck him. I haven't let you come much this week. I think you've earned this one."

"Yes, *Sir*," Cam said, eagerly scooting into position, his smile wide. Ethan crouched between Cam's legs, licking along the thick, erect shaft while Andrew fondled and teased his nether hole, opening it gently with his fingers before lubing his cock head and replacing his fingers with it.

Ethan moaned against Cam's cock as Andrew eased himself carefully inside the hot, tight passage. How many times had he dreamed of this very moment, his cock buried in Ethan Wise's ass? But this wasn't the two-dimensional memory of Ethan as a boy that had colored Andrew's dreams for so many long and lonely years. It was the real man, a thousand times better than any fantasy Andrew could conjure.

"Push back. I want to fuck that hot ass," Andrew said, lust bringing his dominant nature sharply to the fore. Ethan obeyed, slurping against Cam's cock as he thrust back onto Andrew's bone-hard shaft.

Andrew watched Cam's face, which was suffused with pleasure, his eyes closed, his mouth slack. His fingers were buried in Ethan's white-blond hair, holding him against his groin. Andrew thrust hard against Ethan, who bobbed in rhythm against Cam's cock.

All at once Cam's eyes came open, fixing on Andrew. "Please, Sir!" he gasped. "May I come. Oh, god…"

"Yes," Andrew urged, nearly coming himself in the hot grip of Ethan's ass. Cam's head fell back, his body jerking as he came in his lover's mouth.

After a few moments, he opened his eyes and smiled shyly at Andrew. "Thank you, Sir."

Andrew had to have him, that second. He eased himself out of Ethan. "Change places. I want Cam." The subs scrambled to obey and in a moment Cam's sexy ass was presented for Andrew's invasion. Curling his hands into fists, he rolled them in the sexy muscular indentations below Cam's hips, holding him steady as he slid inexorably into the tight, hot circle of muscle.

It was so fucking good, he knew there was no way he was going to hang on much longer. "Jesus," he moaned, "Oh, yeah. Shit, yeah." Ethan's eyes were squeezed shut, his mouth an O of pleasure while Cam sucked for all he was worth. Andrew moved inside him, his balls tightening with the impending climax. With a cry, he shot his seed deep into Cam, gripping his hips as he slammed hard into him.

"Fuck," Ethan cried at the same time, his body spasming as uncontrollable shudders rippled through him.

When Andrew could focus enough to see again and his thundering heart had quieted enough for him to speak, he let a slow, cruel smile curl over his face. Cam had fallen back beside Ethan, a trickle of telltale semen trailing from the corner of his mouth.

"Oh dear. Oh my," Andrew said in a teasing voice, shaking his head. "Looks like someone is going to have to be punished." He tapped his chin with his index finger, pretending to ponder the matter. Ethan would be the obvious choice, having come without permission. But Cam had made him come—he should have pulled back in time to prevent the "accident" from occurring.

"I think," Andrew said finally, "you're both equally to blame, and as such will both be in for some serious cock and ball torture in the dungeon. Is that all right with you?

Eyes shining, the pair answered in unison. "Yes, *Sir*!"

~*~

Andrew came awake slowly, disoriented. The sky outside his window was inky black. He'd been dreaming again, the same dream he'd had about the unattainable Ethan Wise. As he came more fully awake, he heard the soft snoring on his left side and felt the sweet, heavy weight of a warm body on his right.

He laughed softly, full consciousness returned, and with it, a rising joy that made him feel he was levitating just above the mattress. To anchor himself, he reached for both sleeping men, gathering them close on either side. Cam shifted, snuggling against him. Ethan sighed and muttered something in his sleep before subsiding back into his gentle snore.

Andrew leaned back against the pillows and closed his eyes, trying to identify the new feeling coursing its way through him. *I'm happy.* Yes. That was it. It was that simple. It might not last—within a week, a month, a year, he might be alone again and more bereft than he'd ever been when hiding behind his shielded heart.

It was a chance he would take. Life, he knew, didn't come with guarantees. At least he was finally living it.

Made in the USA
Monee, IL
29 February 2024

54189503R00121